Cowboy and the Crusader

by

Gail MacMillan

Cowboy and the Crusader

COPYRIGHT © 2015 by Gail MacMillan

Cover Art by *Debbie Taylor*

The Wild Rose Press, Inc.
PO Box 708
Adams Basin, NY 14410-0708
Visit us at www.thewildrosepress.com

Publishing History
First Yellow Rose Edition, 2015
Print ISBN 978-1-62830-787-0
Digital ISBN 978-1-62830-788-7

Published in the United States of America

The minute Clay Archer stepped into the cell area and saw her sitting hunched up alone on a bench in a corner, his stomach lurched. This wasn't what he wanted, not at all.

"Hello," he said.

"Come to gloat, have you?" She sprang to her feet, eyes flashing her feelings as she faced him through the bars.

"No."

"You have ten minutes," the officer who'd escorted him into the cellblock informed him and left.

"Then why? Do you have some kinky fetish about seeing women held prisoner?"

"You really know how to hit below the belt, don't you?" He removed his Stetson and stood holding it in both hands. "I came to tell you I'm sorry about Jordan…and to see if I could get you released on the grounds of your providing an essential community service…you are the only vet in Chemsly."

"I take it your idea didn't fly with the authorities?"

"No." He shook his head and looked down at his boots. "They said they'd put a notice on the local radio station saying you're unavailable until further notice. It provided the phone number of a vet about twenty miles from here to call in case of an emergency. Furthermore, until this town's one and only judge gets back from his fishing trip tomorrow there's nothing I can do."

"Argh!" Madison's frustration grated out through clenched teeth as she jerked her hands into fists at her sides.

"Well, what did you expect?" Exasperation made him snap back. "You tried to trash my truck."

Praise for Gail MacMillan

"Be prepared to be hooked on the first word of the first page and go on to the next with anticipation. Her stories will live in your heart long after the last page is read."

~*Rebecca Melvin, Publisher, Double Edge Press*

~*~

"Gail MacMillan's stories delight the senses and brighten the dark days of winter like a candle glowing on a windowsill. Best enjoyed while curled up in your favorite chair...with some hot cocoa and a faithful canine companion."

~*Sue Owens Wright, author, newspaper columnist, and two-time Maxwell Medal recipient*

~*~

"Gail MacMillan's stories place you in a well-worn comforting chair. She writes of deep-rooted rural customs and traditions, of her love of dogs and horses. She shows glimpses of truth in revelatory detail."

~*Heather White, Editor, Saltscapes Magazine*

~*~

Other books by Gail MacMillan
Available from The Wild Rose Press, Inc.
Lady and the Beast
Caledonian Privateer
Ghost of Winters Past
Holding Off for a Hero
Shadows of Love
Rogue's Revenge
Counterfeit Cowboy
Heather for a Highlander
How My Heart Finds Christmas
Highland Harry

Dedication

In memory of my parents,
who taught by example the importance
of love and family.

Chapter One

"Are you just going to sit there and let Clayton Archer murder your husband like he killed our father?"

Green eyes bright and hard, Madison Todd faced her sister across a breakfast table littered with half-empty cereal bowls, cold toast, and a pair of coffee cups.

"Maddy, don't start!" Paige Anderson's heart-shaped face and soft blue eyes registered the distress her younger sibling's words caused. "Jordan's fine. Furthermore, Clayton Archer didn't even own the mill when Dad died."

"No, he didn't." Madison picked up her cup and crossed the sun-bright yellow kitchen to look out a window at the plumes of smoke and steam rising from the pulp mill three miles upriver. "But it's been two months since his stepfather died, and he still hasn't bothered to come to check on his inheritance. Mr. Clayton Archer is too busy playing cowboy on some ranch in Alberta. He couldn't care less that his mill is gushing out all kinds of noxious refuse, never mind those poisonous holding ponds somewhere back in the bush…"

"With about as much hard evidence to support their existence as there is to support the reality of a sasquatch or the Loch Ness Monster." Paige picked up a slice of half-hour-old toast and bit into it.

"Okay, why hasn't Environment Canada tried to dispel the stories by doing an investigation?" Madison swung back to face her. "I'll bet a thorough audit of Glendon Forest Products, Inc.'s books would reveal some pretty hefty contributions to local political campaigns."

"That's a serious accusation, Maddy. You should be careful about throwing it around." Paige stood and began to clear the table.

"Is that advice from Paige Todd, chartered accountant, or from Mrs. Jordan Anderson, concerned wife, mother, daughter, and sister?"

"You know I haven't practiced since Daniel and Katie were born." She rinsed the cereal bowls at the sink and put them into the dishwasher.

"Not an acceptable excuse." Madison returned to the table and began to help clear. "The twins are five and in school. They're not babies anymore. What do you plan to do with the rest of your life, clean away the kids' breakfast leavings and drink second, third, and fourth cups of coffee? I know you loved that investigative accounting you were doing before you married Jordan. You were great at it. The Royal Canadian Mounted Police were ready to offer you a permanent position. It's time you got back in the game."

"So I can get myself entangled in your crusade?" Paige turned to her sister and put her hands on slim hips encased in well-fitted jeans. "No, thank you. Most people around here are dependent on the mill for a living. Closing down our one and only industry would be tantamount to turning Chemsly into a ghost town."

"I don't want to close it down...not permanently."

Madison clattered knives and spoons into the dishwasher. "Only a temporary shutdown until the proper anti-pollution devices can be installed and a thorough cleanup of the area is done."

"Good luck. Count Jordan and me out of it. And especially Mom. She's suffered enough."

"That's the whole point, Paige. Mom wouldn't have had to suffer if it hadn't been for Clay Archer's mill. Dad would still be alive, and they'd be retired and happy, and…"

"Madison, for the last time—you have no proof!" Paige shut the dishwasher door with an emphatic thump.

"What is it with you, Paige?" Madison confronted her sister when she turned away from the machine. "Are you taking Clay Archer's side? Why? You didn't know him any more than the rest of us when he lived here. His visits to his mother and stepfather at their estate downriver were always brief, and he hardly ever came into town. I can't even recall what he looked like aside from the fact that he was tall and incredibly skinny…a genuine Ichabod Crane. Most of the time he was either away at boarding school or spending his vacations at some ritzy kids' camp."

"That's just it, Madison." Paige's blue eyes looked squarely into Madison's green ones. "He never had a family life. He was shipped off here and there like a lost package with no return address. Imagine how that must have made him feel."

"Yes, well…" Madison looked out the window and tried to ignore the logic in her sister's assessment.

"Madison, while we were spending all those terrific summers up at the cabin on the lake with Mom

3

and Dad, Clay Archer was off somewhere all alone with his suitcase. Where's your sense of compassion?"

"I guess it left about the same time Mom had to sell the cabin to pay for Dad's treatments." Madison snapped back into fighting mode. "And when she had to go back to work to try to pay off the rest of the bills."

"Maddy, be reasonable. We can't prove it was the mill and its emissions that made Dad sick. Even if they did, Clay Archer didn't own Glendon Forest Products back then. You can't hold him personally responsible. And," she continued, her tone softening, a wicked twinkle coming into her eyes, "what if he's morphed into a tall, dark, handsome cowboy? I remember how you and Dad used to enjoy watching those old John Wayne movies. I also seem to recall that Clayton Archer did have the most amazing blue eyes. You might have noticed if you hadn't been so busy holding hands at the movies with Tommy Mills."

"I was just keeping Dad company while he watched those westerns. Even if Clay Archer had all the cowboy charm in the world, I still wouldn't like him. Furthermore, as you well know, what Tommy and I had was called puppy love. Now we're just good friends."

"Fine." Paige shrugged. "But don't say I didn't warn you."

"Okay, okay. I know when I've hit a brick wall." Madison snatched her jean jacket from the back of a chair. "Ceilidh," she called to her Little River Duck Dog lying in a pool of sunlight near the back door. "I want you to stay with Paige today. I have people to see about this mill business, and I know how bored you get waiting around."

With an eager bark, the little red-and-white dog

leaped to her feet, alert and ready. Paige knelt and gave her a hug.

"I know, Ceil," she said softly. "She tilts at windmills, but we have to humor her."

Ceilidh gave Paige a lick and barked again.

"Really! Making slighting remarks about me to my best buddy?" Madison's sense of humor kicked in as she sat on a chair near the door to pull on her boots. "Well, just for that, Madame Brick Wall, I'll be back…with a chisel and hammer. You may find yourself in heels and a suit, sorting through reams of financial documents that will help to prove my case."

"Maddy…!"

"*You've* been warned," Madison called back over her shoulder as she strode out the door.

Once across the deck and down the steps, she ran through a backyard filled with bright plastic toys and an in-ground swimming pool to where she'd parked her economy 4x4 behind Paige's spanking new fire-engine-red minivan.

As she opened the driver's door, she paused and glanced back at the sprawling ranch-style house that was her sister's home. Jordan Anderson, Paige's husband, made a good salary at the mill—excellent, when you considered his highest academic level was a high school diploma. His income was sufficient to allow them to afford this upscale house and two vehicles. It had also made it possible for Paige to leave her accounting practice and become a full-time mom.

Climbing into the driver's seat, Madison had to admit she understood Paige's reluctance to help in the fight against the mill's emissions. If the plant were shut down, it would be a devastating blow to her family's economy.

I should have come back sooner. She backed out of the drive and headed toward her veterinarian clinic on Main Street. *If I hadn't spent those years in Africa, I would have been able to stop the sickness and suffering here in Chemsly. I might even have been able to prevent Dad's death. And I'd definitely never have met Dr. Jason Kenny.*

The final thought brought a hot rush of anger and chagrin flushing over her. She'd never get caught up in a relationship like that again. No more handsome fly-by-the-seat-of-their-pants guys for Dr. Madison Todd, no siree. When the time came…and it wouldn't be soon…she'd find herself a nice, comfortable man. Someone who'd want children and the kind of lifestyle her sister was enjoying. Someone who loved animals the way she did. Someone who'd be proud to have a veterinarian as a wife. Someone who'd join her in her fight to clean up the Chemsly environment. As her list of qualifications drew to a conclusion, she let a small, sardonic grin curl the corners of her mouth. Someone who'd partner a crusader who occasionally tilted at windmills.

She was stopped at a red light when Paige's description of Clayton Archer's childhood assailed her. Her sister had painted him as a sad little waif. *No, no, no!* Maybe, once, he might have been, but not anymore. Now he owned the biggest killing machine she'd ever encountered. She couldn't afford to let thoughts of his possibly unhappy childhood weaken her decision to put an end to the deadly effects of his mill. And forget that cowboy bit. She was way beyond the point in her life when a good-looking guy in a Stetson and hip-hugging jeans could do anything for her.

As the light changed, she eased her foot off the brake, made a decision, and accelerated.

I'll drive out to see the cabin. That will stamp out any ideas about poor little rich boys, once and for all.

Swinging off the highway, she drove down a chip-sealed secondary road for several miles until she came to a dirt lane that headed into a forest of birches and maples ablaze with autumn hues of reds, oranges, and yellows. A hard knot congealed in her throat. Her father had loved September at the cabin. He'd loved taking long walks through the colorful autumn bush with Sparky, his Border Terrier, scampering by his side. She remembered the exuberance with which he'd greeted the season, decorating the cabin with pumpkins and gourds and refusing to rake up the palette of bright leaves that collected over their verandah and lawn.

"Nature's carpet," he'd say, rubbing Sparky's ears. "I'll clean them up in the spring. Right now, let's just enjoy them."

As she braked to a stop in the dooryard, the place appeared as they'd left it last year. Last year when her mother had been forced to put it up for sale. Molly Todd, with her generous, forgiving spirit, hadn't resented parting with their vacation home, at least not visibly. She'd simply remarked that she was glad she had it to sell to help cover bills. Madison hadn't felt that way, not at all.

She drew another deep breath and walked around to the front of the cabin, her feet swishing through the dry leaves. Under her father's favorite maple, a small grave marker read, "Here lies a faithful friend and companion." Sparky's grave. He'd been nearly fourteen years old when her father died. The loss of his best friend had been too much for the old dog. Within a month he had passed away, too. This had seemed an appropriate resting place for him.

Now it didn't, not at all. The Todds no longer owned the property, and Sparky and his little tombstone would be left to others, to whom both meant nothing. Her vision blurred by tears, Madison turned away from the lake glistening in the October sunlight and strode back to her vehicle.

Clay Archer would pay, she vowed as she slid behind the wheel and wiped her eyes with the backs of her hands. She sucked in a deep breath. He hadn't responded to letters from the Chemsly Citizens' Committee—of which she was vice-chair—but Madison knew she would somehow come up with another method for getting his attention.

****

"Dr. Madison?" The man wearing fishing garb stepped into her office shortly after noon.

"Yes." She looked up from the report she'd been writing. "What can I do for you?"

"I didn't know exactly what to do about something I came across while I was fishing this morning." He fumbled in a pocket and pulled out his phone. "A guy at the gas station up the road suggested you might be the right person to contact. He said you're head of the local SPCA."

"I am." She stood. "Are you here to report animal cruelty?"

"Well, sort of." He flicked through the phone, then held it out to her. "This is what I came across this morning while I was fishing up at what I think is the old

Archer place. I'm not from Chemsly, so I'm not all that familiar with the area."

"Oh, my goodness!" She stared at a pair of horses, ribs showing like curved rails through ragged coats. One a dark grey, the other a smaller sorrel, they stood, heads drooping, against a fence. "You say you discovered these animals at the Archer estate?"

"In a paddock behind the barn. I guess all that's been keeping them alive is the brook that runs through it."

"I'll get right on it." She reached for her jacket. "Thank you for bringing it to my attention. But before you go"—she stopped him as he turned toward the door—"may I make a copy of that photo? I want to email it to someone."

Although the horses' suffering, like all cases of animal neglect or abuse, rankled her to the core, she couldn't help feeling this was just what she needed to get Clay Archer's attention.

She made a few fast inquiries following the fisherman's visit. She learned that a local man, Kelsey Grange, had been Glendon Gregory's stable hand but abandoned his duties shortly after his employer died. The horses had been left on their own.

Her fingers trembling, she sent the information and photo to Clayton Archer.

****

As soon as she'd e-mailed Clayton Archer in her capacity as chairperson of the local SPCA, with a warning of impending charges if he didn't react immediately, she drove out to the estate. The quarter-mile drive from the secondary road to the homestead was potholed and rutted. At its end, a padlocked gate barred her way. Not about to be deterred, she got out and scrambled over it, ripping her jeans in the process.

Damn!

Turning her attention away from the tear, she confronted the dilapidated Victorian manor with its mansard third story standing out bleak against an overcast sky. Its peeling dark red paint, the color of dried blood, sent an involuntary shudder running up her spine.

What a house of horrors. So this was Clayton Archer's home as a child...

She caught herself up short. *Don't start again with the sympathy! Remember Dad. Remember the mill. Remember what might happen to Jordan.*

Walking past the house and around a corner of the weather-bitten barn, she discovered the horses in an over-cropped field exactly as she'd seen them in the photo. Fortunately they'd had water from the stream in which the fisherman had been trying for trout, or they'd have died. Fresh hatred for their owner engulfed her. *How could any human being allow this kind of neglect?*

Stifling her anger, she fed them from a supply of substandard hay she found in the dilapidated barn but decided against putting them inside. It wasn't cold or wet. Another night in the outdoors wouldn't hurt them. She wanted Clayton Archer to find them exactly as they were, to get the full impact of his neglect. As a cowboy, if indeed that was what he was playing at, he'd probably have at least some concern for the creatures. Phone in hand, she moved to take the most compelling photo of the horses' plight she could devise and sent it off to Alberta as a follow-up to her e-mail. If that shot didn't move him to action, nothing would.

She was glad to climb back into her vehicle and head for home. The Archer estate had cast a chill over her. The house looked like something out of the many girl detective novels she'd devoured as a teenager...dark, grim, and mysterious, hinting of nefarious deeds. Of course, such a place always had a dark, handsome, mysterious man as its lord and master.

Well, at least the old manor fitted into that scenario. A dark, handsome man? She scoffed at the idea.

Chapter Two

"Damn it, Clay, this is a bloody disgrace!" Alberta rancher Jim Trent threw the printout of the e-mail containing the photo of two emaciated horses across his desk. "And this woman says they belong to you?"

"Apparently." The six-foot three-inch man standing in front of him ran his hand though dark curls and heaved a deep breath that raised broad shoulders. "They belonged to my stepfather. I told you he died a couple of months ago. I inherited them."

"I thought you said old Gregory loved horses, that they were his one passion."

"According to this e-mail, after he got sick and died, the fellow he'd hired to look after them quit. This pair was left to forage in a pasture that became overgrazed. I imagine all that sustained them was that creek you can see in the background."

"You have no choice, man. You have to go to New Brunswick and see to their welfare."

"I know, but it's coming on to roundup time, and a ranch foreman should be on site."

"I can take care of things here." The big, barrel-chested man stood and faced his employee. "I was a cowboy for a number of years before I took this place over from my father. Clay, let's not haggle. Those horses need you. Take my plane. It's fueled and ready to go. You can leave at first light."

"Thanks, Jim. I'll get ready. I was going to ask to take time off to go down there in the spring, as soon as we finished the branding. My mill manager tells me the operation is running smoothly and doing well financially. I'm planning to turn its profits back into the community by building a heart-and-stroke rehab facility in Chemsly, in memory of my mother."

"Now there's one fine idea." Jim Trent strode over to him and slapped him on the back. "Your mother was disabled by a stroke for some time before she passed, wasn't she? She'd be tickled pink at your plan."

"I think she'd appreciate it." Clay's jaw ticked. "And it would be putting that miserable old man's money to good use."

"Well, you go to it, my boy. And if I can be of any help, just let me know. But I'm hoping that once you put things in order down east, you'll come back out here asap. It's like finding a needle in that haystack folks talk about to locate a foreman with accounting skills, never mind one that can ride with the best of them *and* has a degree in business administration. Damn it, lad, you're a blasted paragon!"

"Hardly, Jim, but I will come back. You've been good to me right from the day I graduated from university. I won't let you down."

"Yeah, well, enough of this talk." Jim Trent turned away and headed back behind his desk. "You have a bag to pack and a plane to fly. I'll see you back here when you get this horse problem settled."

****

"Clay!"

He threw his duffel bag into the plane and turned to see Lacy Trent running across the field toward him,

13

raven hair flying in the wind. "Dad tells me you're leaving, going down to New Brunswick. Something about horses?"

"Yeah, apparently I own a couple that need my attention. I should be back inside of a week."

"Good." She stopped close in front of him and looked up at him with brown, long-lashed eyes. "I'll be missing you, cowboy." Her tone softened seductively over the last words. She put her arms around his neck and kissed him a long, lingering kiss that made him almost change his plans...at least for an hour or two. But he couldn't. That blasted SPCA woman in New Brunswick had sent him another picture of those horses. They looked even worse than in the previous photo.

"Behave yourself while I'm gone." He managed to pull away. "Come on, Chance," he called to the Border Collie that had been using the time to race around the plane.

As he bent to pick up his black-and-white dog and hoist him into the plane, Lacey gave his backside a slap.

"I'll be waiting." She leaned forward over his hip and whispered into his ear.

"And I'll be right back." He placed Chance behind the pilot's seat and grinned. "Hold the thought."

****

Clay Archer tried to relax at the controls of the Piper Cub. Normally he enjoyed flying on a perfect day like this one. Clear blue skies, a nice little tail wind, and Chance sitting behind him in a safety seat.

But this wasn't a pleasure trip, not by a long shot. Not with the local SPCA out for his blood about a couple of mistreated horses, and some environmental group leveling wild charges in an effort to shut down his mill.

His mill. He still couldn't believe it. Overnight he'd found himself sole owner of Glendon Forest Products, a massive pulp-and-paper operation near Chemsly, in northern New Brunswick.

Up until then, his plans had included nothing more than to continue working on the Trent ranch and enjoying Lacey's company. A grin curled one corner of his mouth at the latter thought. *Man, that girl could ride*. But then, as the daughter of a rancher, she'd learned to handle a horse almost as soon as she could walk, she'd told him. Racing her down a trail on his black-and-white pinto, her palomino stretched at a full run ahead of him, had been a rush. And later...

He had to force those thoughts from his mind for the present. As soon as he straightened out this mess in Chemsly, he'd head back to his job in Alberta...and that beautiful woman, her waist-length black hair flowing in the wind.

But first he had to take care of those sad-looking horses. Of all the stupid things to be accused of. Animal cruelty, right! He glanced back over his shoulder at Chance belted into his seat and enjoying the view from his window. There were probably a lot of things Clay Archer could be accused of, but animal cruelty wasn't one of them.

Maybe the SPCA charges had been a good thing. He'd probably have had to come down sometime before spring to confront the annoying group who'd been causing all the stir about emissions from his pulp mill, listen to their complaints, and, if there was any basis to them (which Rick Reid his mill manager had assured him there wasn't), find a resolution. One thing he knew for certain. Nothing or no one would shut down the facility that was going to provide funding for that memorial to his mother.

His thoughts returned to the horses. *Wonder what kind of shape the animals really are in. Hopefully nothing beyond repair. It will be great if one of them is big enough take me for a good gallop once it's back in health. Best way in the world to unwind.*

He looked below at the miles of forest, its deciduous trees turning into a rainbow of reds, golds, rusts, and oranges. *Beautiful country, beautiful day.* Then ahead he saw the tall, smoking stacks of *his* mill.

"We're almost there, Chance," he informed his companion. "Keep your paws crossed that we're not about to be greeted by hordes of placard-waving activists."

He doubted that would be the scenario, since he'd told no one of his coming except that woman from the SPCA. But maybe she'd gotten a group together...

Chemsly airport loomed dead ahead. He spoke into his radio, requesting permission to land, and began the descent.

"Get ready, buddy," he instructed the little dog. "We're heading into turbulence...at ground level."

****

Stetson slapped onto his head, duffel bag slung over his shoulder, Border Collie trotting obediently at his side, he strode across the tarmac in his cowboy boots, headed toward the small building that served as waiting room, baggage depot, and air traffic control headquarters. The day had taken a turn for the dark side. Charcoal clouds rushed to obscure the sun. In the distance, thunder rumbled.

He pulled open the terminal door to let the dog scamper inside ahead of him. Pausing, he looked around. The only person in the grubby little waiting room was a young woman wearing jeans, a faded chambray shirt, a denim jacket, and work boots. Not fancy lady boots but the sturdy, probably steel-toed variety. She looked to be scarcely out of her teens. Auburn hair scraped back into a ponytail without any apparent makeup to enhance natural good looks, she was a cute little thing, but where was that SPCA person? Damn, he hated when people were late. Every minute he was delayed meant those animals out at the estate would continue to suffer.

The cute little thing looked over at him, green eyes widening in—what? Surprise, disbelief, astonishment? He couldn't nail it down. Was she…? No, she couldn't possibly be… She was coming toward him, hand extended.

"Mr. Archer? Clayton Archer? I'm Dr. Madison Todd, the SPCA veterinarian who e-mailed you about the horses. I have my Jeep outside. We can drive out to the estate immediately…if you're willing."

Later he realized he must have extended his hand to meet hers, because he recalled her swift, firm grip for an instant before she turned and looked down at Chance. At the moment he'd been mesmerized.

"Well, hello." She smiled down at the dog with an expression that lighted up her entire face and sent him into a tailspin. She was the prettiest woman he'd seen in months, years maybe. Not beautiful, but pretty in the warm, fresh way that caused him to take a mental step back. He hadn't been expecting anyone like her. An inane urge engulfed him, an urge to gather her into a

17

hug, to nuzzle her neck, to see if she smelled half as tempting as he imagined…

He pulled himself back to reality. *Man, I hope I didn't look as slack-jawed as I felt.* Struggling to get his act together, he ran a hand over his chin and wished he'd shaved that morning.

Chance, aware he was being greeted, snapped into the little trick Clay had taught him. He sat and extended his right front paw, white-tipped tail dusting the floor.

Dr. Madison Todd laughed as she accepted the dog's offer of friendship. The sound had all the natural cadence of brook water bubbling down a mountain stream.

Ah, hell.

"And you are?" she asked the gregarious little dog.

"Chance," Clay heard himself reply flatly. "His name is Chance."

"Hello, Chance." She returned her attention to Clay, her gaze roving up from the dog, bottom to top. He made a stab at guessing her thoughts.

Some guy playing the macho cowboy. I probably should have ditched the hat and boots, but what the hell. It's who I am…now.

"I came as fast as I could," he heard himself explaining.

"Thank you." Her attitude snapped back to cold all-business. "Shall we go? Those animals need attention."

"Sure." He adjusted the duffel bag on his shoulder. "Ready when you are."

****

Outside, he threw his luggage into her vehicle. He let Chance jump into the small rear seat and removed his hat to allow room for him to climb into the front passenger side.

There wasn't much space, but he managed to fold himself into it. As he fastened his seatbelt, he sensed her looking over at him. He glanced across to see a cynical smile tugging up the corners of her lips.

"Sorry. Not much room. I usually travel alone and a lot, so with gas prices what they are, this little vehicle suits. You can put the seat back a bit, but that won't leave much space for Chance."

"No problem." He tried to get comfortable. "We'll manage."

"It must be nice to be able to afford your own plane." She leaned forward and turned the key in the ignition.

"A Piper Cub is hardly a Lear jet." He caught the sarcasm in her words. "And it isn't mine. The owner of the ranch where I work lent it to me when I told him about the horses. He wanted me to tend to them asap."

"Looks pretty posh to me." She glanced at the gleaming blue-and-white plane behind the protective eight-foot chain link fence as they drove through the airport gate. "Your boss must be wealthy. Pontoons and everything."

"Yeah, well, they come in handy if a person has to land on water." He looked over at her and let a grin turn up the corners of his mouth. "There's not always a runway in the bush."

"Right." As she turned out onto the highway, she shot him a look that told him to cool it.

Time to shut the hell up, Archer. Whatever small bit of cowboy charm you may think you have isn't working with this lady.

Focusing straight ahead, he settled back in the seat.

Over the trees surrounding the airport he could see the tall plumes of powdery white smoke issuing from the mill. Shortly he'd be called to task about those emissions. He was ready. He and Rick Reid, his mill manager.

For about five miles they drove in silence through a rural area with small, neat homes scattered among the sunburst autumn colors of maples and birches and the darker, somber greens of spruce, cedar, and pine. Nothing much appeared to have changed since he'd left. Everything looked as bucolic and peaceful as he remembered.

As they arrived on the outskirts of Chemsly, he saw something that hadn't been there before…a sprawling shopping mall. Its field of asphalt parking lot occupied what he recalled had been part of a family farm.

"This is new."

"Mill expansion several years ago brought big salaries to Chemsly." She shrugged. "People needed a place to spend them."

"So Glendon Forest Products has done some good," he muttered to himself.

Staring at the road ahead, she didn't reply.

Now he could see the mill at the far end of town, massive and sprawling, lording over Chemsly like a modern medieval castle. Shortly they were driving down Main Street. Nothing much had changed except for a few new coats of paint and the boarded-up windows of a number of shops he didn't remember as having been previously closed. He wished it made him feel as if he'd come home. Home should bring warm memories. Instead, a hard bitterness welled up.

Finally she turned the 4x4 into a familiar narrow road that led back into the hinterland. Alders and trees crowded in along its sides. Potholes, left over from last spring's thaw and unavoidable because of the road's overgrown condition, made the vehicle bump and jerk. Clay's head hit the roof, and he muttered an expletive.

"Seems this road hasn't had much use lately," he said as a branch slashed across the windshield. "Doesn't anyone come out here anymore?"

"Not that I know of. Kelsey Grange, who was supposed to look after the horses, must have quit shortly after your stepfather died. Until two days ago, it seems no one knew he'd abandoned the horses out here. With the house empty, there was no reason for anyone to visit."

"You're right." He recognized the logic in her words. "We had no visitors besides tradesmen even when we were living here. Makes sense there wouldn't be anyone after the place was abandoned."

"It must have been lonely for you." For the first time since they'd met he sensed a lightening in her tone. *A chink in her armor of anger. Minuscule, but still a chink.*

"Sometimes."

The road took a sharp curve. The faded three-story mansion, its ruddy paint peeling, loomed out of the scraggly clearing ahead. Dark and anachronistic, its silhouette stood out grim and foreboding against the charcoal clouds smothering the blue sky. His gut knotted.

My mother lived out her final years, wheelchair-bound, in this house of horrors, with a miserable bastard for a husband. I swear to God, I'll see his

21

legacy makes the best restitution possible for the years of grief he caused her...and me.

"Gate's locked." She braked to a stop in front of it.

"The estate lawyer sent me this bunch of keys, all neatly labeled." He pulled them from his pocket. "Here it is. The one marked Gate."

He got out, fitted it into the padlock, and pulled the blockage aside on grating hinges to allow her to enter. Once through, she stopped to let him climb back inside the vehicle.

As they drove into the ragged, weed-choked yard, he saw the weathered barn, its door sagging open on a single hinge, a few hundred yards beyond the house. Memories flooded back. It was the same barn in which he'd often found sanctuary from his stepfather's anger, with a battered guitar and a stray cat.

Come on, man, shove those thoughts under a rock where they belong and get on with it. Somewhere around here there's a pair of horses needing attention.

She stopped near the barn. He climbed out and set Chance free. The dog, released after hours of travelling, darted off around the building toward the field behind it.

"Follow your dog," she said, coming to join him on the passenger side of the vehicle.

"Okay." He slapped his hat back on and headed after Chance. She kept pace with him. Once he caught her glancing up at him.

"What?"

"Nothing, nothing." She lowered her gaze.

What had he seen in that look? Curiosity? Interest? A hangover of her previous animosity?

Rounding the corner of the rundown structure, he

saw the pair in the pasture that swept downhill from the back of the barn to a small stream at the edge of the forest. Heads drooping, ribs showing under shabby coats, a tall dark grey and a smaller sorrel stood by the gate near the barn door.

"Hell and damnation!"

"Pretty bad, huh?" He turned to see her staring up at him, green eyes as cold as glass, the enigmatic look of moments previous dissolved into one of bitter disgust.

"Worse than pretty bad." He opened the gate and stepped inside to join them.

"Some people have stones where their hearts should be," the doctor at his side replied. "Let's get them under cover. A storm's going to break any minute, and the last thing these animals need is more exposure to the elements. That barn's not much of a shelter, but it's better than nothing."

"Agreed." He took the gelding by the halter, but when he reached for the mare's he found Dr. Todd already holding it. He gave her a quick, affirmative nod. Together they headed into the stable.

****

"Damn!" he exploded when he saw the filthy box stalls. "We'll have to tie them in the walkway. We can't put them into those messes."

"They'll be fine out here." She reached for a rope hanging from a ring on the wall. "We can feed and water them now and muck out those boxes later."

"Right." Clay pulled himself out of his rage and realized the practicality of her statement. "Food and water. There used to be a good hand pump around the side. I'll see if it's still working." He picked up a pair of buckets.

"This hay is usable." She pointed to the opened bale she'd used to feed the animals. "It isn't the best, but until we can get something better, it will have to do."

"Okay, but as soon as we do what we can for them, I'm getting on the phone to order some decent feed and bedding. You probably know where I can buy that kind of stuff?"

"Definitely."

Something brushed against his leg, and he started. Looking down he saw her, a grey cat staring up at him, golden eyes glowing in the dimness of the old building.

"Hello." He hunkered down to greet her. With a yowl she jumped back.

"Hey, lady, I'm not going to hurt you. You been staying here alone? Well," he continued as he noted her distended belly, "not alone all the time, apparently."

"She looks as if she could stand a good meal, too." The doctor had come to stand over them. "Being that pregnant probably slows her down, makes catching food a bit of a chore."

"I'll see that she has it as soon as I can get stuff delivered."

"I think she'll survive a bit longer. Anyhow, she'll be safe here in the barn."

"Yeah, safe." He'd felt relatively safe here in the barn whenever his stepfather's rages had lashed at him in the house. He and another grey barn cat…

"Well." He stood, mentally brushing aside those memories. "We'd better get on with our work."

****

When both animals were in decently clean box

stalls and had been fed and watered, Clay heaved a relieved breath. At least now they had shelter and food. But what if he hadn't come? What if Dr. Todd hadn't insisted? He turned to look at her. Even dusty and disheveled from barn work, her hair escaping from its ponytail, she was an eyeful. He watched her give the wasted mare a kiss on the nose.

A tad unprofessional but shows a caring heart. He brought his thoughts up short. *Don't go getting involved.* The warning slashed across his mind. *A woman like Dr. Madison Todd has to be spoken for. Her kind doesn't go running around loose for long.* In an effort to alter his train of thought, he reached for the hayfork and started to shove more food in front of the gelding.

"No, no." She stopped him. "Too much all at once, in their condition, isn't good. They have to be brought back gradually."

"Okay." He put the fork aside and grinned at her. "You're the doctor." He drew a deep breath and leaned against the wall, arms crossed on his chest to survey the neglected stable. "Man, this place is rundown." He looked up into the dark rafters above him. "I hope the roof doesn't leak. There's a fair number of shingles missing."

"Even if it does, these animals are better off than they were an hour ago. Thank you."

Catching a note of softening in her tone, he turned to look down at her. Her shirt had a wet smear across the front where one of the horses had nuzzled her, there was a streak of something he didn't have to struggle to identify on the ankle of her jeans, and a cobweb had snagged in her hair. Still she looked great.

"It's a lot less than what should have been done weeks ago. Now I suggest we make a run for the house. Unless I'm badly mistaken, that's hail I hear hitting the roof. Those clouds looked as if they were carrying a whale of a storm. And listen to that wind."

He was right. The moment they stepped outside, a barrage of hailstones propelled by gale force wind assaulted them. Under heavy cloud cover, daylight had darkened to a threatening charcoal. Together they pushed the barn doors shut and barred them.

When they paused to catch their breath, he saw her shiver. She wasn't dressed for this kind of weather. Pulling open one side of his jacket, he drew her inside its shelter. She flinched and started to shrug away, but a vicious gust sent ice pellets into a stinging, blinding attack. Sheltering her face, she huddled against him.

He caught a whiff of something light and pretty and feminine that had nothing to do with the barn they'd just mucked out. His body reacted.

Get a grip, Archer. You're only the proverbial any port in a storm.

"Let's go," he shouted above the roar of the wind. She nodded her head against his shoulder. Together they ran for the house, Chance at their heels.

At the door they separated as he dug into his pocket and again found his key ring. He selected one, shoved it into the lock, and turned it to the left. The door swung inward on protesting hinges. They scuttled into the kitchen as a jagged bolt of lightning brightened the room with an accompanying boom of thunder so intense the old house shook.

"Good Lord!" She'd been more startled by what she'd seen in the flash of illumination than by the storm, he guessed from her inflection.

"Yeah, good Lord." He suppressed a more colorful expletive and borrowed hers as he gazed around the unpleasantly familiar room. "Welcome to my home."

It was like stepping back in time, back at least a hundred years. The place appeared to be much as it had been when he'd lived there during those brief visits between vacation camps and boarding schools. In the scant late afternoon light from the room's two long, narrow windows, he saw the big wood-burning cookstove, filthy from neglect, the rust-stained enamel sink with taps high on its backboard, the open-fronted cupboards that held an assortment of chipped dishes, and the floor covered with cracked linoleum. The place smelled stale and musty and sour.

"Come on." He headed into a dark passageway that led toward the front of the house. "Let's see how the rest of this place has fared."

The remainder of the ground floor, which consisted of a dining room, parlor, and an office-den, was furnished with dusty, threadbare Victorian furniture and rugs. Dampness had worked on the faded wallpaper, making it peel and curl. Cobwebs hung thick and ubiquitous.

"You can't stay here." Her words reflected dismay. "Everyone in town knew your stepfather was miserly, but I don't think many people were aware of how he actually lived. He never invited people to visit, and his wife was never…"

"And his wife was never allowed out of his sight." His response held caustic bitterness. "Don't be afraid to say it. I know how he treated my mother."

"I'm sorry."

The sincerity in her response made his throat thicken. During his years in the house, he'd had little genuine kindness, his mother afraid to defend him against his stepfather. Now, even these few meager moments in this setting affected him more deeply than he cared to acknowledge.

Man, what a wimp.

"Yeah, well." He struggled to brush aside the emotion. "It's over and done, so let's move on."

"Agreed. We'd better leave, before the storm gets any worse. There's a decent bed and breakfast in town not far from where I live." She turned to go back in the direction of the kitchen. "I think they'll accept Chance. If they don't, he can stay with me until you're settled."

"Thanks, but no thanks." He stopped her with the words. "This is my home. I intend to stay here. Someone has to tend those horses. But you should get on the road. Driving in a storm like this can be tricky."

Another bolt of lightning illuminated the room, with thunder again so intense the old house shuddered.

"This is a bad one," she said. "Dry lightning. The bush has been like tinder all summer. A fire started in the back country could be disastrous."

"The hail has let up, but you're right. There hasn't been a drop of rain." He paused and looked out a window to where high winds whipped up dust devils in the storm-induced twilight. "You say it's been a bone-dry summer?"

"Desert-like. God, why doesn't it rain?" She whirled to stare out the window, arms crossed on her chest, her body rigid.

"Weird weather," he commented and tried to make his tone flat and casual as another gust hit the old house, which creaked in response, its windows rattling. "Maybe you should stay until morning. It's dark now, and the lane isn't exactly in prime condition."

"That would hardly be appropriate." She turned back to face him, green eyes cold. "The sooner I leave, the better. The storm seems to be intensifying."

She strode out into the shadowy recess of the foyer and pulled back the bolt on the front door. When she opened it, a gust of wind, dust, and dry leaves swirled inside, but she lowered her head and ran out into the thickening darkness.

"Wait!" He started after her, but by the time he'd reached the verandah she was in her vehicle and had started the motor. He watched through the encroaching night, swirling leaves and clouds of dust rising from the dry yard as she spun the 4x4 around and headed for the lane that led into the trees and back to the main road.

As she reached the drive's entrance, the gale shrieked to new heights. Clay heard a cracking, splintering sound as a huge poplar tree at the top of the lane was blown over and crashed across the road inches in front of Madison's vehicle. As she braked to a skidding halt, he vaulted over the verandah railing and sprinted toward her.

"Get out!" he yelled, pulling open the driver's door. "Get out before another one comes down!"

She sat staring straight ahead at the massive tree blocking her path.

"Get out!" Clay leaned across her, turned off the engine, released her seat belt, and pulled her out. "Come on, run! We have to get back to the house!"

Half dragging her, he ran back to the porch, up the steps, across the verandah, and into the foyer to slam the door behind them.

"You could have been killed!" He held her by her shoulders and stared down into her pale face.

Under his hands, her body shuddered.

Shock.

He released her and strode up the rickety old stair steps two at a time to the upper story. He found a patchwork quilt on the bed in the spartanly furnished room that had once been his and gave it a flap. Freed dust motes whirled in the stale air. Bundling the bedding under his arm, he made his way back to where she remained in the foyer, arms wrapped around her body.

"Sorry about the dust and stale odor." He drew the quilt around her shoulders.

Forcing what he hoped was a reassuring grin, he held his hands under her chin for a long moment, looking down into her face.

Hell, she's pretty.

She returned his gaze for a moment before he felt the tug at the bedcover.

Backing off. Okay. I'm a gentleman. I can respect that.

"Come into the parlor." He turned to lead her into the room to their left, snapping a light switch as they passed one. Nothing.

"Guess that was too much to hope for, but the fireplace is likely still operational. I'll build a fire. Got a match?" He tried to lighten the mood with the corny old intro line to take his mind off her sexy appeal as he hunkered down and began to ball up papers from a woodbox beside the hearth.

She guffawed. "No!"

"I'll have to see if my stepfather left any lying around." He returned his attention to the fireplace, adding kindling and logs. The chore completed, he stood to confront two hurricane lamps on its mantel.

"Ah, ha!" He picked up a small bottle from beside one. "I knew there had to be matches close by in some kind of container to keep them safe from mice."

He checked the oil in both lamps and lighted first one, then the other. The pair cast eerie shadows over the dilapidated room. *Damn it, that didn't help the ambience, not one bit. Made it more spooky, if anything.* He struck another match and bent to apply it to the papers under the kindling and wood in the fireplace. Straightening, he stepped back to watch as flames erupted.

"You're adept at fire building."

As he turned to face her, he was glad to note the shakiness had gone from her voice.

"Yeah, well, ten years of working on a ranch that consists of miles and miles of nothing but miles and miles give you a chance to learn to survive *sans* electricity." He drew a deep breath. "This old place isn't quite as bad with a bit of warmth and light. You stay put while I run out to your SUV and get my luggage. I have a cell in it. You can call whoever is expecting you and explain the situation."

"I have a phone." She reached into the pocket of her denim jacket. "A vet has to be accessible to her patients."

"Sure, I should have thought of that. I'll just run out and get my own stuff."

Through howling wind and flashes of lightning, he made the trip to the 4x4 and back in what he considered

31

record time.

Damn, what a weird night! I've been out in lots of storms, but never one like this...bone dry and threatening as hell. A great night to spend in this setting for a horror movie.

He arrived back in the house, duffel bag in hand, to find her curled up in a corner of the threadbare sofa talking on her phone. Holding a finger to her lips she signaled him to silence.

He shrugged and obeyed.

Talking to her boyfriend? Doesn't want him to know there's a man around? Damn, maybe it's her husband. Maybe she's married. I didn't see a ring, but maybe in her line of work she can't wear one. Better shelve the hormones, my man, until you get a few more facts about Dr. Todd.

The idea made something in his gut jerk. Picking up one of the hurricane lamps, he left her to it and headed for the kitchen to see what provisions might be available.

As he made his way down the hall, accompanied by weaving shadows cast by the lamp in the darkness and the banshee howling of the wind around the decaying mansion, he let a sardonic grin tip his lips.

A perfect setting for a gothic novel, the old-fashioned kind his mother used to read, where the beautiful heroine got trapped in a moldering manor with a dark, handsome, mysterious man.

His mother. Her memory sobered him. Living in this decrepit horror, she'd had no escape other than into the romantic fantasies of books. She'd deserved so much more.

Although that rehab center he was planning

wouldn't make up for her years of suffering, it would be something.

Nothing and no one would stop him from seeing it was built.

Chapter Three

Curled up in the corner of the old sofa, Madison pulled the musty quilt more securely about her shoulders. She was trembling again, and that was the last thing she wanted Clay Archer to see. He'd think she was weak, vulnerable after a little scare.

Or maybe he wouldn't. He'd already given her one major surprise. The moment she'd seen him swing long, jean-clad legs out of the fancy airplane, slap that Stetson on his head, and begin to stride toward her, all six feet three inches of him, broad-shouldered and narrow-hipped, in cowboy boots, she'd realized that Ichabod Crane, over the past ten years, had metamorphosed into someone who could do a Calvin Klein ad that would leave women drooling. A day's worth of stubble had only added to the rugged earthiness of his appeal.

Oh, God, why did he have to turn out to be the handsomest cowboy I've ever seen? Why couldn't he have stayed like I remember him? Paige will have a field day when—if—she meets him.

When he'd stepped into the terminal, he'd looked at her with blue eyes so intense and mesmerizing that, for a moment, she'd forgotten he was her sworn enemy. She'd had to conjure up ugly images of the mill and those toxic holding ponds to keep her cool, and had to avoid glancing at him for more than an instant during the drive out to the estate.

To top it all off, he was so damned affable. And he had that adorable dog. And he had seemed genuinely concerned about the horses, and…

"How do you feel about beans and peaches, washed down with an excellent vintage?" He came back into the room, a bottle of wine in one hand, two water glasses in the other. "I've got a fire going in the kitchen stove, and some canned beans I found in the cupboard are warming. This, I discovered in a side cabinet with the tinned peaches."

"Are you sure it's wine?" She looked at the bottle skeptically. "I'd heard Glendon Gregory was a vehement teetotaler. Maybe it's cleaning fluid stored in a wine bottle."

"Sealed with a cork? Unlikely." He placed all three items on a table by the sofa and proceeded to fill the glasses to the halfway point. "The old man probably received it as a gift and kept it squirreled away for years, too miserly to give it to someone who might enjoy it. These elegant drinking receptacles are evidence. Not a wine glass in sight."

He handed one to her and picked up the other. "Here's to you, Dr. Todd, for saving two innocent animals from probable death." Lowering his glass toward her, he grinned.

She hesitated, then held hers up to his. "And to you, Mr. Archer, for coming to their rescue."

Their gazes met as their fingers touched. In that instant, lightning flashed and thunder exploded with a blast that shook the old house to its foundations. Something zapped through Madison like an electric shock.

Good God, what was that?

He was staring down at her, a strange expression that bordered on shock crossing his face. Had he felt it too? An offshoot of the lightning? It must have been.

As the sounds of the storm rumbled to a mutter, she lowered her glass, took a small, quick sip, and ordered the butterflies in her stomach to light somewhere.

"Yeah, well, thanks, but I don't think I deserve any accolades just yet." He tasted the wine and backed off a couple of steps. "Make yourself as comfortable as possible while I check on supper." He glanced down at his glass. "This isn't bad, I guess. Hasn't turned to vinegar anyway. I'm no connoisseur. Beer drinker most of the time."

With a quick grin that sent more sensations charging uninvited through her body, he turned and left the room.

Wrapping the old quilt more securely about her, Madison gazed into the fire, still unnerved by what she'd experienced. *Maybe this old place really is haunted, and a crazy spirit zapped me with some weird charge to amuse itself.*

Stop it, Madison Todd. Don't be ridiculous. You always did have a colorful imagination. It was just the storm and the electricity it's generating. You probably rubbed your feet on this old carpet on the way in, and that, combined with what's happening outside…

"Dinner is served." He returned carrying a tray with four bowls, two of them filled with baked beans, the other pair with peaches, spoons and forks beside them. He smiled at her, blue eyes making something inside her flutter—*damn it*—again.

"Thank you." She glanced up as he placed the meal

on the table in front of the fire. "You shouldn't have bothered. As soon as this storm lets up and we can clear the road, I'll be leaving."

"Clear the road? With what? It'll take a chainsaw and a vehicle a lot bigger than your mini-SUV—and broad daylight—to get that tree out of the way. No, Dr. Todd, I'm afraid there's no way you'll be leaving this house of horrors until morning. Did you manage to get in contact with anyone on that cell and let them know where you are?"

"My sister, Paige." She didn't add that she'd told her she was spending the night in her clinic with a sick dog. Paige, like herself, had an active imagination. No sense giving her sister nightmares about Madison murdering Clayton Archer in his sleep.

"Good. Your family knows you're safe and sound. Anyone else you should inform?"

"My mother. She's an OR nurse at the hospital. I left a message on her home phone." The same lie she'd given Paige.

She began removing the food from the tray, setting out their improvised meal.

"That's it? No partner, no significant other?" The tone of his voice made her glance up at him.

Why is he looking at me like that...as if he's really interested in my answer?

"No." She picked up a bowl of beans and settled back on the couch. "I'm a career woman."

"Oh."

"You have something against single working women?" The question came out sharper than she'd intended, too full of defensive annoyance.

"No, no." He held up his hands in a gesture of

surrender as he sat down beside her. "I'm unattached myself. I understand. A job can take up a lot of a person's time."

Lacey Trent, but nothing serious there. Both of them had agreed. Just some fun.

"Yes, I imagine running Glendon Forest Products is time consuming." She let a little acid drip from her words as she spooned into her beans.

"I wasn't referring to my inherited position," he said, picking up his bowl and stirring. "Although it will probably keep me busy now that I'm here. I meant my job in Alberta, as foreman on the Trent ranch."

"A ranch foreman?" Astonished interest escaped into the words before she could stifle them. She hadn't considered that coming from a wealthy family he might have a real job. She'd thought he was living an extended vacation on some sort of dude ranch.

"Yeah." He looked over at her. "Great job."

He took a spoonful and chewed as he continued to look over at her, a slow grin starting at the corners of his mouth.

Stop it! Don't look at me like that!

She took a gulp of wine and choked.

"Maybe you're a beer drinker too?" he said as she set the glass aside and struggled to regain her composure.

****

As they finished their makeshift meal, Madison glanced out the window into a night that was black as pitch. The thunder and lightning had abated without a single drop of rain being shed, but the wind still howled around the old house. She hoped no fires had been started back in the bush.

"This should be time for coffee." He stood and began to gather the dishes back onto the tray. "Unfortunately, the water's been turned off, so unless one of us is willing to jog down to the pump at the barn, we'll have to settle for a second glass of wine."

"Okay by me."

"Good. I know the gallant thing to do is to volunteer to go, but I'm glad I don't have to."

She glanced up at him, and the twinkle in those remarkable eyes held her as surely as if they'd been exerting a physical grip.

"And I don't have to prove myself a strong, independent woman—which, by the way, I am—by offering to go." She pulled herself out of the spell she seemed to be under and matched his tone.

"A meeting of minds. A decent start to our relationship." He put the last of the dishes and utensils on the tray and picked up the wine bottle to replenish their glasses.

"Relationship?"

"Sure. We're going to have a working relationship for a while, I hope. You are willing to be my vet and help me get those horses back to health, right?"

"Yes, of course." A slight flush slid up her face as she realized she'd misconstrued his words. *Don't let him notice. Please don't let him notice.*

"Good. You can start by giving me the names of people to contact in the morning for feed and shoeing." He sat down beside her again.

"Definitely." She tried to stifle the feelings his closeness flashed over her. "Lander's Agricultural Supplies can provide grain and good quality hay. A friend of mine, Tom Mills, is the best farrier for miles.

I'll give you both phone numbers before I leave."

"Thanks. And thanks for agreeing to care for the horses."

"My job." He probably didn't know she was the only vet in town, but still she appreciated his vote of approval in the face of her being responsible for threatening him with animal abuse charges.

"Then that's settled. I'll also need to be put in touch with some local contractors and get their bids on repairing this place. Do you know any?" He looked down into his wine and swirled it slowly about in the glass.

"I know a couple." She took a sip, stood, and went to stare into the flames crackling on the hearth. "If you like, I'll call them tomorrow morning."

"Great." He got up and went to join her. "Winter's not that far off, and that old barn doesn't look as if it can stand much more weathering."

"You're planning to keep the horses here?" She was surprised. She'd expected his visit would be brief, just long enough to place the animals in proper care.

"For a while, until I've had time to decide how I'm going to deal with all this." He waved a hand to indicate his surroundings. "Home, sweet home. Yeah."

Bitterness bristled from his words, startling her. Something about this weird old house had brought it out as instantly as a whiplash, had changed the charming, affable man into a cynical creature with eyes as cold as winter ice. His expression hardening, he raised his glass to his lips and finished off his wine in a single quaff.

"Now I'm going back to the barn to see how my charges are doing." He set the empty glass aside.

"Enjoy the fire and the wine."

"I'm coming with you." For some inexplicable reason she didn't want him to go out into the night in that frame of mind. She hurried on when he paused to look at her, surprise in his expression. "Now that you've retained me as your vet, I'll be keeping close tabs on them." She couldn't let him see even the smallest hint of caring or concern. Clay Archer was the enemy, for God's sake.

"Okay." He rooted through his duffel bag. A moment later he pulled a flashlight out of its depths. "We'll go down to the barn together."

****

Ten minutes later, she felt his gaze on her as she knelt to examine the mare's hoof by the light of his torch. He still had no idea she was the person responsible for declaring his mill deadly dangerous. She wondered what he'd say when he discovered the truth.

"Just needs a good farrier." She pulled herself out of her musings and straightened up to face him. "I'll see Tom comes out as soon as possible."

"Great." He looked and sounded relieved, his former good nature apparently having returned. "Now we'd better get back to the house. Chance will be worried. I don't often leave him alone, and these are new and…strange surroundings."

"No sign of the cat." She looked around as they left the box stall.

"A bit shy, I'd guess. Hiding probably. I'll bet she shows up when I've got food for her."

Together they left the building and headed back to the house. The wind had abated and the thunderclouds rolled away. A slice of moon struggled into view. In its eerie half light, the old house stood out stark and spectral against a sky full of scudding black clouds.

"Spooky, isn't it?" His tone indicated he was grinning as, together, they closed the barn doors and put the bar in place. "Maybe I should call it Halloween Haven."

"If you're of a fanciful turn of mind." She pushed her hands into her pockets and hunched her shoulders as they started toward it.

"Are you?" He paused beside her as they reached the steps leading to the back door.

"Hardly. I studied science for years to become a vet. The paranormal isn't highly regarded in that discipline."

"Right." He pushed open the door and stepped aside for her to precede him. Inside, she led the way back to the parlor. The hurricane lamps still burned on the mantel, but the fire on the hearth had fallen to embers.

"How about throwing on another log while I look around upstairs for a couple of blankets and pillows?" he said. "This is the best place for us to spend the night. From what I could see when I went to get that quilt, the bedrooms aren't very inviting. You take the couch. I'll sleep in that chair."

Before she could protest, he was on his way upstairs, the beam of his flashlight making a weaving path of illumination in front of him.

****

A thin, dusty beam of light from a six a.m. sunrise brushed his face. Clay Archer opened his eyes. For a moment, he thought he must be still asleep. The Victorian parlor seemed more like the setting of a nightmare than reality, a place of bad memories, at the very least. Then he saw her asleep, curled up on the sofa, a faded quilt clutched to her throat. And remembered.

Man, she's pretty. The thought kept recurring. He came fully awake and pulled himself upright in the chair where he'd spent the night. Her hair, released from its ponytail, fell in a tangle of auburn curls and waves over her shoulders. It softened her features and made her look, in sleep, so innocent and unspoiled she might have been a princess in a fairy tale.

Stop it! Crazy fantasizing isn't helping. She's far too appealing without me inventing stupid scenarios around her.

With a stifled groan, he struggled out of the chair and stood. From a rug on the floor beside him, Chance whined and stretched, white-tipped tail beginning to flog.

Clay put a finger to his lips, a sign the little dog understood to mean quiet. He picked up his boots from where he'd discarded them by the fire the previous night and headed for the kitchen on stockinged feet. Chance danced at his side.

He lit the woodstove, then rummaged through the cupboards until he found an ancient percolator and a decrepit-looking can of coffee.

Man, I need a cup so strong a spoon will stand in it.

"No way around it, buddy," he informed the dog as he sat down to pull on his boots. "We'll have to go to the pump at the barn for water."

He opened the back door and let Chance gallop down the steps and across the yard. The sun rising red

43

and raw in a dusky haze promised another bone-dry day. He remembered his mill manager's comment about how the entire area had had a tinder-dry summer and Rick Reid's concern regarding the possibility of forest fires.

"We've already had a few small ones," Reid had told Clay when he phoned him from Alberta. "So far, we've been able to contain them, but if a really good blaze got started in the back country, it could wipe out a major source of our raw products."

As he walked toward the barn, Clay scanned the trees surrounding the estate, relieved to see no columns of smoke rising into the murky crimson sunrise. Seemed they'd been lucky last night.

He kicked a small dust hummock and watched it explode into a greyish-brown cloud. Looking toward the dried-out, over-cropped pasture behind the barn, he marveled at how the horses had managed to survive.

Once in the building, he moved between the stalls, giving both animals the amount of hay Madison had recommended. The gentle, affectionate demeanor of both horses amazed him, considering the neglect they'd suffered. As he pumped water into buckets, his thoughts reverted to his years on this estate, and his stepfather. Those horses might forgive neglect and worse, but he couldn't. He looked around for the cat, but again she didn't appear.

When he'd finished, he filled the percolator and headed back to the house. He'd muck out the stalls later. Right now he had to impress a lady. He grimaced as he ran a hand over the stubble on his chin and jaw. A shower and a shave weren't possible in that dilapidated house. He'd have to make perfect coffee and be charm on the hoof if he wanted to get her attention.

Yeah, right.

He liked Dr. Madison…a lot. She had a sincere, no-nonsense approach to life that made him respect and admire her. But he sensed there was much more to her than met the eye. Beneath the businesslike façade he perceived the lady had some raw places. The way she'd jerked away from him on the slightest physical contact said a lot. Something or someone had left her scraped and bleeding inside.

He'd like to help her heal, he thought, as he started up the steps into the house. He'd at least like the chance to try.

He stepped into a kitchen warm and alive with the crackling sounds of the newly lighted fire in the cooking stove. Beside it, Madison Todd sat on a wooden stool, pulling on her boots. She glanced up as he entered, and a smile flashed across her face. It disappeared as quickly as it had come, and she returned to her task.

A reflex? Okay, I'll take whatever I can get…for now.

"Good morning," he said, crossing the room to place the percolator on the stove. "I went down to the barn to get water for coffee and ended up tending the horses. Took me longer than I'd planned."

"I thought that might be where you'd gone." She got up and went to where the innards of the coffeepot and a squashed bag of coffee sat on the cracked counter.

She pulled open a few drawers until she found a spoon, looked it over critically and, with a resigned sigh, shrugged, wiped it on the sleeve of her shirt, and proceeded to measure coffee into the percolator's perforated cup.

She's known rough times. Times without the niceties of life. A sense of kinship nipped at him.

She'd made an attempt to recapture her hair into a clump at the back of her head, but it had proven renegade. Tendrils fell forward around her face and down her neck, and she looked like a heroine in a movie adaptation of one of Jane Austen's novels. Even in rumpled shirt and jeans Dr. Madison Todd could hold a man's interest.

Mrs. Bennett wouldn't have had any trouble marrying this one off.

He remembered how straight her hair had been when she'd met him at the airport and realized she must have had it styled that way, probably with considerable effort, judging from the present riot of curls.

"Why did you have your hair straightened?"

She hesitated.

Ah, damn. Probably another one of those questions you're not supposed to ask a woman. Way to go, Archer.

Finally, as she turned and went back to the cupboard, she answered.

"Curly hair isn't in. Don't you read magazines or go to movies?"

"Not women's fashion publications, and I'm not a movie fan. But I do know what makes a woman attractive, and, believe me, the way your hair is right now does it for you."

She placed two cracked mugs on the counter, hesitated, then turned to him.

"Thank you." The response was sharp, as coldly

polite as any he'd ever received. "Now let's get down to work. I'm going to start calling some of the people you'll need if you plan to keep the horses here, and try to find someone to clear the drive so I can get to my clinic."

"No need to do that last bit. I'll call Rick Reid, my mill manager." *Fine, if she wants to keep it strictly business. I'll go along with the plan...for now.* "I'll ask him to send out a couple of guys with a truck and chainsaws to clear the drive. Getting you back to your patients is top priority."

****

"Rick? Clay here. I need a favor." He leaned against the porch rail as he spoke into his cell. Madison had gone down to the barn to check on the horses while he made arrangements to have the drive cleared.

"Sure, just name it, Boss." The mill manager's good ol' boy twang came across loud and clear.

"I need a couple of guys with a truck and chainsaws to clear my drive." A grin tugged at his lips. He liked Rick's down-to-earth, good-natured personality. "I'm out at the estate, and last night's storm blew a pretty big tree down across the driveway. We've been trapped behind it ever since."

"Out at the estate, you say? I had no idea you were comin' to Chemsly so soon. But unexpected doesn't mean unwelcome, not by a long shot. Good to have you handy, Boss. I'll send a couple of my best woodsmen out right away. But you said 'we.' You bring someone with you from Alberta?"

"No. Dr. Todd, your local veterinarian, came out yesterday to check on a couple of horses and got trapped here by the storm."

Gail MacMillan

The line went dead silent.

"Rick, you there?"

"Yeah, yeah, sure. Are you sayin' Madison is out there with you, that she spent the night? Just exactly when did you get here, Boss?"

"Yesterday, and it's not like that. She sent me an e-mail, as chairperson of your local SPCA, about a couple of neglected horses out here at the estate. She threatened to have charges brought against me, so I decided to come down to see for myself. She picked me up at the airport yesterday afternoon, brought me out here. Then that storm came up, felled a tree, and trapped her."

"So she threatened you." The mill manager paused, then added with a chuckle that sounded eerily Machiavellian, "Madison can be one devious darlin'."

"Why do you say that?" Figuratively Clay's hackles rose.

"Got you here way ahead of schedule, didn't she? You hadn't planned to come until spring, as I recall."

"The horses got me here. She was simply the informant."

"Okay, okay. I'm hittin' on a tender spot. All I'm sayin' is watch yourself around the good doctor. She's full of surprises, and not always pleasant ones."

"Advice taken." In an effort to still the chafing his manager's words had started in his mind, Clay hurried on with the conversation. Damn. He'd been right when he thought her too good to be true, but right now he didn't want to hear any more. "When can I expect that help?"

"Pronto, right away. And I'd like to meet with you real soon, Boss. When can we get together? You name the time and place, and I'll be there."

"How about Wednesday morning, say around ten thirty, your office at the mill?"

"Sounds good. Anything else?"

"I could use some wheels, if you've got any to spare."

"Sure, sure. Oh, and, Boss?"

"What?"

"I feel I have to repeat my warnin'. Don't turn your back on Dr. Todd. She can be one connivin' cookie, appearances to the contrary."

He punched off before Clay could question or respond.

****

A half hour later, two trucks arrived. The one leading the way was a dusty woods vehicle with chainsaws and gas cans in the cargo bay, the second a fire-engine-red, state-of-the-art, king cab 4x4 pickup with "Glendon Forest Products Inc." emblazoned on its sides. Showroom perfect, it gleamed with superfluous chrome. Both vehicles braked to a stop at the fallen tree.

Chance prancing ahead of them, Madison and Clay came down the verandah steps and crossed the yard to greet the men as they stopped at the fallen tree.

"Morning," Clay called to the man wearing jeans, steel-toed boots, and a plaid shirt as he got out of the woods truck. "Thanks for coming so fast. Dr. Todd has to get back to her patients."

"Yeah, well..." The man slapped on a hard hat. "Rick said we had to rescue you pronto. I'm Bob Davis, and the guy driving your truck is Austin James."

"Clay Archer." He rounded the end of the tree

blocking the road to extend his hand. "You probably already know Dr. Todd."

"Oh, yeah, right, sure." One corner of his mouth quirked upwards. "Morning, Doc. Everything okay?"

"Bob, I really have to get to my office." Madison cut the man short. "Can you please just get on with the job of clearing the road?"

All business, no soft edges. Is that what Rick Reid meant? If that's all...

"Whatever you say, Madison. Come on, Austin." He turned to the other woods worker, who'd gotten out of the red truck and come to join him. "Let's get rid of this mess. Oh, by the way, if you didn't get what I meant just now about Austin driving *your* truck," he continued as he and his companion each reached for a chainsaw, "that 4x4 is for you, Mr. Archer. Rick said you needed wheels."

"A bit of overkill, but tell him thanks." Clay glanced at the fancy vehicle. "And my name is Clay, not Mr. Archer."

As he and Madison headed back to the house, the men bent over their chainsaws.

"Take care, Clay," Bob Davis called after them.

Glancing back, Clay saw the two men exchange knowing grins before their equipment roared into action.

****

An hour later, he stood on the front step and gave a farewell salute from his hat brim as Dr. Todd drove down the newly cleared drive. Bob Davis and Austin James also watched her leave. There'd be gossip at the mill today, but there was nothing he could do about it. Protesting would only make things worse.

Well, so what? Even though nothing happened, or even if it had, we're both over twenty-one, consenting adults. Big deal.

Unless Madison Todd is something a lot different than she appears to be, muttered a nagging little thought that had begun to flitter around in his head after Rick Reid's warning.

Stop it. Useless speculation. Time will tell. Let it go.

"Thanks, boys," he yelled out to them. "Want a cup of coffee? It's not great, but it's hot."

****

A half hour later, he watched from the front verandah again, this time as the workers drove away. Good men, both of them. He'd enjoyed talking to them as much as he enjoyed conversations with any of the men he supervised on the Trent ranch. They liked their work. Being in the woods agreed with them, they'd told him. Neither could imagine being cooped up in an office, and he understood. He couldn't do that, either. His job as foreman did include a fair amount of desk work, but there was always the prospect of a gallop in the fresh air when he'd finished. He missed Apache and urging the horse into the all-out run the pinto enjoyed as they raced Lacey Trent and Gold across the acres of ranchland.

Lacey. He hadn't given her a thought since he'd met Dr. Todd. The idea paused him. Then he shrugged and headed into the house. She probably hadn't wasted a whole lot of time thinking of him, either. More given to action than speculation, Miss Lacey Trent kept her life full and busy.

He crossed the foyer, then stopped to peruse the

51

faded, threadbare parlor where his mother had spent most of her last months and years.

In the shadowy room, he remembered the last time he'd seen his mother alive. Abby Archer-Gregory had been in her wheelchair, lines of stress and suffering disfiguring her once beautiful face, but the moment she'd seen him, a smile as bright and wonderful as a rainbow had lighted up her countenance.

"Clay, sweetheart, how good to see you." She'd held out a hand, and he'd crossed the room in long strides to drop on one knee beside her chair and take it. "How well you look. I'm so glad."

"Sweet Jesus!" He sank into a chair and doubled over, the tightness in his chest overwhelming him. He struggled to take deep breaths, to get his feelings under control.

He'd let her die here. He should have taken her away…somewhere, anywhere.

He hadn't been there for her while she'd lived, when she'd needed him. He'd let Glendon Gregory drive him away, make him think the money the old man had to spend on her care and treatment was more than Clay could provide, more important than a son's presence. He, Clay, had been young, had allowed himself to be persuaded to make the wrong decision.

Now he had to do all he could to make it up to her. He'd honor her memory in the only way he could think of, the way he'd decided shortly after he'd learned of his inheritance. He was going to use every cent of profit from the mill to build the finest stroke rehabilitation center on the East Coast, and no crazy environmentalist was going to stop him.

Chapter Four

Another kind of determination, mingled with frustration, welled in Dr. Madison Todd's chest as she drove away from the Gregory estate. She'd come so close to liking Clayton Archer she couldn't believe it. Maybe it had been because of his concern for the horses and her personal comfort. Or maybe it had been his crooked grin that had made her feel as if they were friends, the kind of friends who shared and cared. Or maybe it had just been something as simple as his killer-handsome cowboy looks.

Oh, please, don't let it be that last thing! That's so high school. Damn it, where did that Ichabod Crane person go?

It didn't matter. She had to put a stop to those feelings, and fast. Otherwise she'd be useless when she faced him in battle across a boardroom table. The fact that those two men from one of his woods crews now knew she'd spent the night at his estate wouldn't help. In a small town like Chemsly, that kind of news spread like wildfire. She'd have to contact all the members of the Chemsly Citizens Committee and set them straight as soon as possible. It would be time-consuming, time a busy person like herself could hardly spare, but it had to be done.

In town she stopped at her sister's to pick up Ceilidh. Paige was in the throes of getting the twins off to school.

"How's the dog?" Her sister paused long enough to ask about Madison's fictional overnight patient.

"Dog? Oh, yes, the dog. Fine. We'll talk later. Right now I have to get back to the office. The poor little guy needs me. Only took a minute to run over here to get Ceilidh."

She gave Daniel and Katie each a quick hug and kiss. "Come on, Ceil," she called. "Got to run."

"I'll call you," were Paige's parting words as Madison and her dog ran out to the SUV. Madison was sure she would. She'd made a stumbling mess of the sick dog lie.

But she hadn't lied about the busy morning part. She drove to the bungalow she rented on the edge of town at the top of the speed limit, showered, and dressed in fresh clothes. Forty-five minutes later she pulled into her parking space beside the former shoe store that now served as her office and surgery.

The property had been inexpensive to rent. Most downtown businesses in Chemsly had moved out to the new mall when it opened four years ago. Others that hadn't relocated had been forced into closure by chain stores with cut-rate prices.

Stepping from her Jeep, she heard her stomach rumble. That less-than-stellar cup of coffee in Clay Archer's kitchen hadn't been much of a breakfast. She let Ceilidh into her office and headed for the coffee shop next door. She was paying for a coffee and bagel when Rick Reid's voice made her freeze.

"Mornin', Miss Madison. What's this I hear about you dallyin' all night out at that old manor house with the new boss man? Shame, shame, shame."

She whirled to find the mill manager standing close behind her, a crafty grin creasing his face. In his mid-thirties, Rick Reid, a good-looking, sandy-haired, rugged outdoorsman, had hazel eyes that could twinkle with either good will or sly malice. At the moment, they glinted with the latter.

"It wasn't like that," she hissed. "The tree that fell in last night's storm trapped us, and you know it. Keep your voice down."

"Now, now, don't go gettin' all haughty." Taking a firm grip on her elbow, he drew her away from the counter and the too-interested waitress. "Actually, you should be thankin' me for not tellin' him…yet…exactly who you represent. Poor innocent soul, he thinks you're just a nice little lady who cares about horses. I'll give you a little more time to circle your wagons before his pretty picture gets dirt all over it."

She stopped short. "Why?"

"I'm not about to tell him on the phone and miss seein' his face when he finds out. No way. I'm gonna be there in the flesh for that auspicious moment."

"You're a genuine bottom feeder, you know." She shrugged free and glared up at him, hoping all the contempt and anger burning her insides blazed from her eyes.

"Come on now, Madison. Let's not resort to name-callin'. I could fling a few myself, missy, if I weren't a gentleman."

All bantering and good humor vanished as he leaned closer. "Mind where you tread, Dr. Todd. Remember, aside from tellin' him about your Erin Brockovich imitation I've got one hell of a trump card I can throw on the table if you force my hand. And while you might be willin' to face up to it yourself, your family could have one big heap of trouble dealin' with it."

As quickly as it had vanished, Rick Reid's grin returned. He winked at her and strode out of the shop, whistling, hands stuffed into his pockets.

****

She'd donned her white lab coat and was getting out the files of her first patients when the bell over the front door jingled. She looked up to see Tom Mills in jeans, T-shirt, and work boots come striding into the office, two cups of coffee in a cardboard tray and a brown paper bag in hand.

"Tommy, hi!" She was glad to see the tall, good-looking farrier.

"Hi, yourself, Doc. Thought I'd drop by for breakfast and get the scoop on this Clayton Archer guy before I head out to do his shoeing. Said you gave him my number, when he called a few minutes ago, and that he'd be grateful if I got out there asap. I see you've already been to the coffee shop." He indicated the cup and bagel on her desk.

"That doesn't mean you can't join me." She took a seat behind her desk and indicated a chair in front of it. "Pull up a seat."

He pushed the chair closer to the desk with his hip. Settling into it, he placed the coffee and sack between them.

"So what's he like, Maddy?" He punched the tab on the lid of the Styrofoam cup and took a sip before continuing. "A real piece of work like his stepfather? The only good thing about Glendon Gregory was the fact that he cared about his horses. Until he died, that is, and Kelsey Grange gave up looking after 'em."

"Actually"—Madison opened her coffee and slanted him a teasing smile—"he's deceptively nice."

"Deceptively nice?" Tom dug into the paper sack and pulled out a chocolate-coated doughnut. "Those two words don't fit together, kid."

"No, they don't," she agreed. "But then, a lot about Clayton Archer doesn't fit."

"Still butt-ugly, though, right?" Tom's dark eyes brightened with interest. "I was a little worried when he said you'd given him my name last night. And when I phoned your house about nine in the evening, there was no answer. I didn't try your cell. I know that's for emergency use."

"I was tending a dog." She bit into her bagel and refrained from elaborating. She knew Tom's reaction wouldn't be pretty if she told him she'd spent the night with Clayton Archer. His quick, hot-tempered jealousy where Madison was involved had been one of his weaknesses ever since they'd been in grade school.

"So what's he like?" Tom, with his usual single-mindedness of purpose, got back to his inquiry.

"Like I said, deceptively nice." She leaned back in her chair, coffee in hand. "He appears genuinely distressed about the condition of the horses. His call to you is evidence of that concern."

"But you don't trust him, right?" Tom bit into his doughnut.

"Not as long as he continues to operate that noxious mill and does nothing to stop its poisons from belching out over our town."

"Good. I was afraid he might turn out to be charm and sophistication on the hoof." Tom picked up the remains of his breakfast and arose. "After all, old Gregory did send him to all those fancy schools. I'd better get out there and see to those horses. Talk to you later."

He was heading for the door as Madison's first patient of the day, a lame German shepherd dog, arrived with its owner.

"I'll bet he's still butt-ugly, though," Tom called back as he went out.

Madison couldn't contain a grin as she invited Piper and his master into her examining room. Tommy Mills was in for one colossal surprise.

Chapter Five

Clay Archer stood at the bottom of his verandah steps, waiting, when Tom Mills drove his king cab 4x4 into his dooryard and braked to a halt. As the lanky farrier swung out of the driver's seat and faced him, Clay saw what he read as astonishment flash across his visitor's face.

"Clayton Archer?" The man overcame whatever surprise he may have experienced as he advanced toward Clay, hand extended, an amused grin sliding across his face. "I'm Tom Mills. Maddy said you wanted your horses shod."

Maddy. A nickname. This guy and Dr. Todd have more than a nodding acquaintance. An unpleasant feeling pinched his gut. *Jealousy? Get rational, Archer. You haven't known the woman twenty-four hours yet.*

"Good to meet you." He accepted the farrier's hand. "Thanks for coming so promptly. I hope the feed and grain Dr. Todd ordered arrives as fast. Those animals need all the help they can get, and the sooner the better."

"Kelsey Grange is a bum." Tom leaned back against his truck and adjusted his baseball cap over his eyes. "The only reason old Gregory tolerated him was because he works cheap. You planning on keeping him?"

"With a recommendation like that?" Clay grinned.

"Hardly. And especially not after what I've seen here."

"You want me to ask around for a new stable hand?"

"I'd appreciate it, but take your time and find me a good one."

"What'll you do in the meantime? Put up with Kelsey?" Tom crossed his arms on his chest and looked steadily at him from under the peak of his cap.

"Handle the barn work myself." Clay returned his steady gaze. "I have to hang around awhile anyway to meet with some ditzy environmentalist who's convinced my mill is murdering the entire population of this valley."

"Ditzy, eh?" Tom turned and climbed back into his truck. "I'll drive down to the barn and get started. I have three more places to visit this morning."

Is he smirking? Why?

****

"Let me give you a hand." Clay came out of the mare's stall, tossed a forkful of manure into the old wooden wheelbarrow, and headed back to where Tom had secured the stamping, snorting gelding in the crossties. He leaned the fork against the wall and moved to the animal's head.

"He's pretty raw." Tom stepped back as Clay took the big grey's halter. "Green broke, no better, I'd guess. Be careful."

"Easy, easy." Clay spoke softly and placed his free hand gently on the animal's neck. "Take it cool, and Tom here will have your feet feeling better in no time at all. Deal?"

As he spoke, the gelding slowly calmed. By the time he'd finished speaking, the animal had reduced his antics to soft blowing and a bit of slow tap dancing.

"Good boy." Clay patted him on the neck. "Now relax. This won't take long. I'll let you go for a gallop in the pasture afterwards." He turned to Tom. "You can start shoeing. I'll stay with him…in case he gets antsy again."

"You've got a way with horses." Tom adjusted his cap and set to work. "Where'd you learn?"

"Believe it or not, at boarding school. We had a riding instructor who employed a kind of horse-whisperer philosophy. These last ten years, I've been working on a ranch in Alberta. Big place. Over a hundred head of horses."

"Yeah? Well. Huh." Tom put his hand gently on the horse's left shoulder, then ran it slowly downward until he could pick up its hoof.

The gelding shuddered, but when Clay spoke softly to him he quieted.

Tom glanced up questioningly at Clay, and he grinned down at the farrier. "Go ahead. Scout's okay now."

"Scout?"

"This morning I found his registration papers in a desk in the house. He's a registered quarter horse with a long name that ends up as Scout."

"Good name. I like it."

Clay scratched Scout behind an ear as the farrier began his work. He liked Tom Mills.

"Did you know Maddy was a championship rider back in high school?" The farrier surprised him with the fact as he trimmed the animal's front hoof. "She had a whole bunch of ribbons and trophies before she went off to college and vet school."

61

"Is that right? Quite a lady, Madison Todd."

"Sure is." Tom Mills' eyes narrowed at he looked up at Clay. "There's not much she can't do when she puts her mind to it. Never underestimate her, buddy."

There it was again. A warning. What was up with Dr. Madison Todd? She definitely didn't look like an ax murderer or anything half as bad. Yet already two men had hinted at something that would surprise him. Was there something sinister about the woman he was finding more and more irresistible?

****

At six o'clock that evening, Madison turned the last curve of the drive and braked to a surprised halt.

The scraggly yard around the decrepit Victorian mansion had been mowed. A shiny new lawn tractor was parked near the front step, beside the bright red pickup with Glendon Forest Products clearly labeled on its doors.

Down by the barn, lumber and other building materials were piled beside a display of fresh tire tracks that indicated there'd been a goodly amount of coming and going already. Clay Archer had been busy. Apparently he could make things happen when he chose to. Hopefully he'd react the same way about his toxic mill.

She'd been surprised when he called shortly before noon and invited her to dinner that evening. She'd expected he'd be too busy with business to socialize, much less prepare a meal for a guest.

At first she'd hesitated, unsure if she wanted to get more involved with Clayton Archer on a personal basis. Then logic had kicked in as the old cliché about catching more flies with honey than vinegar echoed through her mind.

"Please," he'd said when she paused, and she sensed that appealing crooked grin in the word. "You were a great help to me and my horses. I'd like an opportunity to show my appreciation. I promise I'll have something better than beans."

"Okay," she'd said finally. Better the devil you know than the one you don't—a second old adage echoed through her brain. "Six o'clock okay?"

With a sigh she eased her foot off the brake and drove through the gate that was now invitingly open. *Here goes.*

As she stopped near the back door, he stepped out onto the porch, his dog at his heels, to greet her. Her breath caught in her throat. Dressed in a light blue shirt and jeans that looked as if they'd been custom made to hug his flat belly, slim hips, and long legs, shaved and with his curly hair combed into the best semblance of order she guessed possible, Clay Archer was definitely in resolve-breaking form. Worst of all, he was wearing cowboy boots. The mill and its noxious emissions slipped to the back of her mind as she allowed herself to enjoy the view.

"Hello." He came down the steps to open the door of her vehicle. "Glad you could come."

He saw Ceilidh and his welcoming grin broadened. "And who are you, pretty lady?"

"This is Ceilidh." Madison swung out of the 4x4. The little red-and-white dog bounded after her. "I hope you don't mind that I brought her along. She's been cooped up in the office all day. I knew she'd enjoy an opportunity to stretch her legs."

"Seems you made a good decision," he replied as

Chance, who'd been sitting on the verandah, bounded down the steps to join them. The two dogs, after a bit of preliminary sniffing, dashed off toward the barn together. "You didn't tell me you had a Little River Duck Dog."

"The subject didn't come up. I'm surprised you'd recognize her breed. There aren't a lot of them around."

"One of the teachers at one of the boarding schools I attended in Nova Scotia had one. Great little dogs." He drew a deep breath. "I was going to suggest you come down to the barn, to see if I'm doing okay, but you're definitely not dressed for it."

She saw warm approval in his eyes as his gaze slid over her. Assisted by a soft tangerine-colored sweater that cried out "touch me" and a pair of beige pants with a fit she'd been proud of since the day she'd purchased them a month previous, the honey thing appeared to be working. She'd even let her hair go natural and allowed a few curls to escape from the coil at the back of her head. Bit by bit she was finding out what he liked and preparing to use it against him.

"These old things?" She flicked a hand down her front and favored him with what she hoped was one of her most disarming smiles. "Barn clothes in the making. Let's go."

Inside the stable she stopped short, amazed. Fresh bales of hay and bags of grain had been stacked against the back wall beside several shining new water buckets. The cobblestone corridor between the stalls had been swept clean, and there'd been an obvious beginning made at tidying up the rest of the place and discarding the rubble.

"Looks good," she managed over her surprise.

"It's a start." He shrugged. "Tomorrow a construction crew will begin to fix it up properly. New roof, repaired stalls, paint. Now come on. Take a look at Candy and Scout."

"Candy and Scout?" She followed him to their stalls, across the walkway from each other.

"They're both registered quarter horses. I found their names on some papers in the house," he said, opening the door of the gelding's stall. "How am I doing, Doctor? Will these conditions temporarily meet SPCA standards?"

Clean sawdust provided bedding, there was hay in the manger, and a shiny aluminum water bucket hung on a C hook in one corner. As Scout moved toward her, Madison saw Tom's handiwork on his hooves and also that the animal had been curried in an attempt to refine his neglected coat.

"I'll need your advice on graining." He was watching her closely. "I don't want to risk colic or anything like that. I've never dealt with undernourished horses."

"Of course." She patted the gelding's neck. "But you appear to be doing fine. I see you're utilizing materials from your mill." She brushed the toe of her shoe through the sawdust bedding.

"May as well. Absorbs moisture and odor better than straw."

He'd followed her into the stall. He stopped close behind her, so close that if she turned she'd be inches from him. Something fluttered in her chest.

Ducking under the horse's neck, she came up on the far side and smiled over at him. "No further evidence of the cat?"

"No actual sightings, but apparently she's still hanging around." He indicated two stainless steel bowls in a corner near the back of the barn. One held water, the other was empty. "She must have surfaced long enough to have a meal."

"You intend to take care of her?" Although she tried to shove it away, something about his concern for the stray cat touched her.

"She's in a family way." He shrugged. "I figure she could use a little TLC."

****

He was doing just fine with the house, she discovered when she entered the kitchen and saw a gleaming new stainless steel refrigerator-freezer side-by-side combination, electric stove, microwave, and dishwasher. The place had been cleaned and, although still in need of cupboard doors, countertops, paint, and flooring, it looked reasonably hygienic.

"You have a terrific janitorial service in Chemsly," he answered her unvoiced question. "And a fast-delivering appliance store. I've even got electricity and water. By tomorrow night I'm supposed to have a land line, wi-fi, computer, and satellite television."

"Are you always this efficient?" she asked, running a hand over the gleaming stove.

"Yeah, well, I do like my creature comforts. Living outdoors a lot of the time on the ranch gives a person a deep appreciation for electricity and indoor plumbing. Let me show you the rest of the place."

He led her through the hall to the parlor. The curtains, opened wide, let in evening sunlight to reveal the results of diligent cleaning. The hearth had been swept clean and the makings of a fresh fire lay ready.

Next he opened the door opposite the fireplace, to reveal a dining room where an antique table, chairs, and sideboard had been polished until they shone. Dishes, cutlery, and a pair of candles waiting to be lighted sat ready for dinner.

"Amazing."

"Thanks. And all without a woman's touch." She caught his teasing glance and forced a smile.

"I won't show you the upstairs. It's clean but pretty grim and tattered. I need new bedding and towels. In those departments I could use a feminine touch."

"I'm sure there are stores in the mall that can help you." Catching the hint of appeal in the remark, she turned the trend of the conversation. "Maybe we should get to that dinner you promised. I have a couple of patients to see around eight this evening."

"Sure, sure. Right this way." He escorted her into the dining room before heading back to the kitchen.

"Dinner was prepared at a great little restaurant I discovered next to the appliance store," he said, bringing a Caesar salad to the table. "Next time, after I'm settled in, I'll do the cooking. In the meantime, take-out lasagna and rolls are coming right up."

As if there'll be a next time. Once you find out what I really represent, you'll never want to see me again.

"That would be nice," she said. And smiled.

****

After dinner they sat on an old porch swing and watched shadows reach from among the trees on the lane and deepen. The dogs, exhausted from running about the estate, lay at their feet. They talked of animals and renovations. He was clever and witty and downright charming, Madison hated to admit. He even seemed caring and sincere.

"So you think I should try to keep the Victorian ambience as much as possible." His words reflected that he was taking her suggestions about the old house seriously. "Any ideas as to how I can manage it? Where would I get the stuff? Most of the furniture is pretty threadbare and scratched up, not to mention the peeling wallpaper and mangy rugs."

His description of the carpets made her grin.

"Mangy?"

"Yeah, well, I'm not up on the latest lingo to describe dilapidated houses."

"Then I guess 'mangy' will do." She leaned back and felt herself relaxing. "Auctions, flea markets, antique stores in the city… It would be fun. I've always dreamed of renovating an old place like this." *Damn it, keep your visions and enthusiasms to yourself. That came off sounding like you're interested in his plans.* "You could hire an interior decorator and tell her what you want." *There. Fixed.*

"I suppose I could, but I don't know how comfortable I'd be with some strange woman running around the place with swatches of this and that, and books of wallpaper samples."

"Up to you." She shrugged. *How was that for cold and disinterested.*

"Temperature's dropping," he said. "Let's go inside. I'll light a fire in the parlor."

Good. He got the message.

"I really have to be going." She looked at him in the soft September twilight. A wish that he wasn't owner of Glendon Forest Products swept over her, and she hurried on with an explanation. "As I've said, I have a couple of patients to see this evening."

"Right. Next time we'll make it a night when you don't have appointments."

He held out a hand to help her up. Focused on getting away, she accepted automatically. As he drew her to her feet, her foot stumbled on a loose plank. He caught her in his arms in time to save her from tumbling down the verandah steps.

Startled, she looked up at him. In the soft country twilight, intense sapphire eyes gazed into startled emerald ones. Magic slid over the moment. Slowly, carefully, he brought her full length against his body and lowered his head to put his mouth over hers. Her entire being did a sharp uptake. Clay Archer was kissing her, kissing her in a way that made her insides flutter as if a thousand butterflies were having a party.

Her knees turned to jelly. Lost in overwhelming sensations, she met his ardor completely, fully, her arms going about his neck, letting him engulf her in his desire. It had been so long since she'd been in a man's arms, felt the hot strength of desire emanating from a male body hard against her own. Her heart raced, pounding off like a filly freshly freed into pasture after a long, cold winter of restraint. She floated, soared with him against her will, against common sense.

"Man!" When he finally let her come up for air, he looked down at her, his expression as astonished and breathless as she felt. "What was *that*?"

Madison stared up into those killer cowboy eyes and knew exactly what it had been.

"One very big mistake." She wrenched free, and headed down the steps toward her Jeep. "Come on, Ceilidh. It's time we headed home."

Chapter Six

Clayton Archer couldn't sleep. He kept tossing and turning, memories of Dr. Madison Todd driving him nuts.

What *had* happened on that verandah, he wondered as he punched his pillow into yet another shape. He'd come on with a knee-jerk reaction just because a beautiful woman had bumped into him. He'd never behaved like a macho idiot in his life before, and thirty-two didn't seem to be a reasonable starting point. He was lucky she hadn't decked him. Given the strength required in her work, she probably could have done it pretty darn good.

But she hadn't. He stretched out on his back, fingers laced behind his head. In fact, she'd met his impulsive passion with right-back-at-you fervor. The remembrance made him grin up at the cracked ceiling revealed in the moonlight gliding in through the ragged curtains at his window.

And one of her ambitions was to renovate an old Victorian house. He had a Victorian home that needed renovations. He wanted to pick out paint and rugs and wallpaper with her, not with some artsy decorator who had no more idea than a June bug about what made him tick. He wanted to watch Dr. Madison Todd's green eyes sparkle as each room became what they'd planned together.

Damn it, it was way too soon to start thinking about her like this. He barely knew the woman. Beyond one really hot kiss, that is. And she'd crunched that experience pretty fast by running away like Cinderella from the ball, without even leaving a glass slipper of hope. Or one of those fancy tan-colored sandals she'd been wearing that made her feet and ankles look sexy.

She'd even labeled the kiss a mistake. *Damn!* He rolled over and pounded his pillow again. With a defeated sigh, he stretched out on the bed. Dr. Madison Todd would drive him crazy soon, if he wasn't careful...like she nearly had on the verandah earlier.

He drifted off to sleep, thinking the ride he'd taken on that notorious mare Crazy Daisy back on the ranch would be nothing compared to what he'd experience if he tried to keep company with Madison Todd.

****

He awoke early the following morning and, after a quick cup of coffee, slapped his Stetson on his head and strode down to the barn carrying a blanket. He'd decided to try Scout. He'd seen a couple of dusty old saddles in the barn, and a pair of bridles. If the mice hadn't done a number on them, he'd be all set.

He refilled the cat's bowls with food and water. While the mare and gelding were munching the fresh hay he piled into their mangers, he cleaned the stalls and made another round of inspection. Once he was convinced Scout's appetite had been satisfied, he led the animal out of his stall and put him in the crossties.

"Easy, boy," he said softly as he placed the folded blanket on the animal's back. Scout wriggled his hide and blew softly as he accepted the improvised saddle cloth.

"Great. You're used to it. We're off to a good start, buddy." Encouraged, he picked up a saddle, blew dust from it, and slung it up onto the gelding's back.

The cat emerged from a dark corner and sat down to watch.

"Good morning," he said barely glancing at her. "So you decided to show yourself. Guess the provisions are softening you up."

She opened her mouth wide and meowed.

"Is that a thank you? Very nice." He paused, then slowly hunkered down, facing her. "Would you like to come over here and be friends?"

Again the wide-mouthed response.

"Okay, okay." He stood and returned to his task. "When you're ready." *Like the good doctor. No more advances until she indicates she's ready. Damn it, where had that thought come from?*

Ten minutes later, he started Scout off at a walk down one of the trails that led into the woods behind the estate. The gelding had responded well to his commands when he'd taken him into the pasture and lunged him on a long line before mounting. He'd been pleased, and so far the ride was going well. Tomorrow he'd try Candy. If she proved manageable, he'd invite Dr. Todd to go riding with him. Tom Mills had told him she'd been a competitive rider in high school. Someone like that never lost their love of horses or their ability to manage them. Anyhow, it was the best idea he could come up with to get her to come out to the estate again. Pleased with the prospect, he nudged Scout with his heels as the trail opened into a meadow.

He touched his heels to the gelding's sides and was exhilarated as the animal responded quickly and willingly.

This guy has a bit of training under his ragged coat. Maybe Candy has, as well.

The trail emerged into a meadow crested by a rolling hill. Clay reined Scout to a halt and drew a deep breath. He caught a whiff of something unnatural and unpleasant in the air and saw a faint haze veiling the sun. He wondered if it was from his mill, then stopped himself. Hadn't he been reassured all was well there? Why go looking for trouble?

He glanced around and allowed the few good memories he had of this place to surface. It was beautiful country. He'd loved it when he'd lived here as a youngster. He could have been happy if it hadn't been for the grasping miser who'd married his mother and made both their lives agony.

He exhaled and tried to breathe out all the old hurts and animosities. He had to shove the past away and get busy with the present and future. His thoughts were turning to Madison Todd when his musings were interrupted as a pair of riders galloped over the rim of the hill.

A man and a woman, he decided, adjusting his hat and narrowing his eyes against the sun. A man on a big white animal, a woman on a gleaming black.

It can't be. But, yes, damn, it is. Tom Mills and Dr. Madison Todd.

They reined to a stop when they saw him, then proceeded in his direction at a trot, both horses prancing, showing off their health and vitality. Clay adjusted himself in his shabby saddle and patted Scout's shaggy coat.

'You'll look as good as those guys soon, boy," he

assured the gelding.

Scout snorted.

"Morning." Tom drew rein in front of Clay and touched the peak of his baseball cap. "Great day for a ride."

"Sure is." Clay leaned on his saddlehorn and forced a grin. "Good morning, Doctor. Fine mount you've got there."

"Thank you." Madison quieted her prancing animal. "She belongs to Tommy. They're both dressage horses."

She was looking at him—no, staring at him. At his hat? Now, what was that about?

"Impressive. You two ride together often?" He tried to keep a casual conversation going and avoid puzzling over what her focus on his Stetson meant.

"Not often enough." Tom patted his mount's thick, arched neck. "Maddy's pretty busy these days, what with her practice, and the SPCA, and…"

"Tommy!" The admonishment snapped from Madison like the crack of a whip.

"Well, isn't it time he knows how things stand? No sense his wasting time howling at the moon."

"Damn it, Tommy!" Madison swung the black around and headed back the way they'd come at a full gallop.

"Seems the lady isn't happy about something you said"—Clay squinted at the farrier in the sunlight—"or were about to say."

"Yeah, well, Maddy doesn't like anyone to speak for her. Rides well, doesn't she?" He gestured at Madison's retreating form.

"Very well."

"I taught her when we were both teenagers. We've been riding together ever since." He paused and faced Clay with narrowed eyes. "I wouldn't want anything to change that." He swung his cavorting horse around. "So don't get any ideas. Remember I'm the guy on the *white* horse."

He touched his heels to his mount's sides. The animal half-reared before it galloped off in pursuit of Madison.

Clay watched until they were out of sight, then turned Scout toward home.

"Seems we have our work cut out for us, boy."

****

Clay arrived at the mill a half hour before his scheduled meeting with Rick Reid. He wanted to take a private stroll around the facility. He'd had no difficulty gaining admittance. The fact that he was driving a truck with the company logo on its doors had been his passport.

As he walked through the vast, noisy, high-ceilinged rooms filled with massive equipment and unpleasant odors, he realized he knew little about the pulp-and-paper industry. The machinery looked in good condition, and the workers willingly busy. Most of them greeted him with a grin and a wave even though they could have no idea who he was. A number of them, he noted, were Asians.

Is the mill doing so well Rick Reid can't find enough local workers?

At ten a.m. Clayton Archer presented himself to Rick Reid's secretary in his mill manager's outer office.

"Mr. Archer. Of course." Her face flushing, she scrabbled to her feet and hastened to the door to her

75

right. "Come this way, sir. Mr. Reid is expecting you."

"Thanks." He flashed what he hoped was a reassuring smile as he passed her and stepped into his manager's office.

In contrast to the other parts of the mill he'd visited, this room was an oasis of tranquility and cleanliness. Its entire back wall consisted of floor-to-ceiling windows facing east to catch the morning sun. Thick tan rugs, chrome-and-glass desk and tables, and an impressive chocolate-brown leather couch with four matching armchairs, as well as a well-stocked bar, completed the ambiance of tasteful sophistication. It smelled fresh as a spring breeze.

As Clay entered, a tall, sandy-haired man who'd been seated behind the shiny desk in front of the massive windows stood. Right hand extended, an affable grin lighting up his face, he strode across the room to meet his new boss halfway.

"Clay, boy, good to see you! Chrissy, get us some coffee, that's a good girl. And mind you make it Starbucks. None of that instant dishwater."

"Yes, Mr. Reid." The secretary scurried away.

A good old boy. Clay evaluated his manager. *A bit over the top, but a whole lot better than some stuffed shirt. I can relate to this guy.*

"Great to finally meet the new boss man face to face. Have a seat." Rick Reid slapped him on the shoulder and indicated a chair in front of his desk. "Although I must say your call came as a surprise the other day. I had no idea you were comin' to Chemsly. But unexpected doesn't mean unwelcome. Sit down, sit down. Chrissy will be back with that coffee in a minute. Or maybe you'd prefer something with a little more bite to it?" He indicated the well-equipped bar in a far corner.

"A little early for me, thanks. By the way, it wasn't necessary to send that fancy truck. Any set of wheels would have been okay."

"Not necessary?" The mill manager took a seat in the high-backed executive's chair behind the desk, as soon as Clay was settled, and slapped his hands palms down on the surface in front of him. "Of course it was. You're the boss around here. You gotta look the part. Now, which will it be first, a tour of the plant or a look-see at the books?"

"A tour." Clay glanced around the opulent office. "I'll leave the books to an accountant. What I really want to do," he continued as he settled in his chair, elbows on its well-padded arms, fingers steepled into a pyramid, "is to set up a meeting with the head of that citizens' committee that's out to shut us down. I assume I'll find Dr. Steven McLean at the local hospital?"

"That's right, but he's just the figurehead of the group...looks good to have an MD as chairman, don't you know. About all Steve does for that crowd is lend his name and sign letters. As the only surgeon in town, he doesn't have time for much more. The real mover and shaker behind that troublesome bunch is a lady I believe you're already acquainted with...our local veterinarian, Dr. Madison Todd."

"Madison Todd." A bucket of ice water hurled onto his privates couldn't have shocked him more. "Are you sure?"

"Sure a' shootin'." A corner of Rick Reid's mouth quirked up in a sardonic grin, a wicked twinkle brightening his eyes. "She's been makin' like Erin

Brockovich ever since her father died and she came back here to live. A real caped crusader, that's our Maddy."

"She's the reason I came down here now." *Hell, he'd been getting all hot and horny for his archenemy.* "She sent me an e-mail on behalf of the local SPCA, informing me that I had a pair of badly neglected animals on my property and I'd better get my sorry ass down here or face charges—not in those exact words, but ones that brooked no refusal."

"That's Maddy, all right." Rick Reid chuckled. "Tough as shoe leather, pretty as a picture, and devious as hell."

"She and her group have laid some pretty serious charges against the mill." Clay pulled himself up straighter in his chair and looked across the desk at his manager. He hoped the galling anger he was experiencing didn't show in his face. "I received one hell of an accusatory letter from that crowd a few weeks ago."

"Yeah, well, Maddy lost her dad last year. He was only sixty-one. His death hit her hard. Guess she had to blame it on someone, and the mill came in handy." The mill manager shook his head and looked down at his desk. "She and old Dan were real close. The man actually took typin' lessons the year before he died, for God's sake, just to be able to e-mail her in Africa."

"Africa? What was she doing in Africa?" Facts about Dr. Madison Todd were surfacing hot and heavy, stinging like shards of hail.

"Teachin' impoverished farmers how to care for their animals, offerin' medical advice and treatment." He waved a dismissive hand as he got up and went to look out the big window behind his desk. "She and some medical doctor went out there for a few years after she graduated from veterinarian college. So you see"—he swung back to face Clay and stuffed his hands into his pockets—"our Maddy has a history of takin' on hopeless causes."

"Then you believe her charges against the mill are groundless?"

"Hell, yes. This place has been government-inspected from stem to stern. It's as safe as a lily in a duck pond. Maddy's just actin' out her hurt and pain. I wish she hadn't brought you down here for nothin'."

"It wasn't because of the mill that I came," Clay reminded him.

"No, that's right, isn't it?" Rick Reid shook his head and grinned ruefully. "Neglected animals. That Maddy. Quite a gal. Never misses a beat."

The office door opened, and Chrissy entered balancing a tray of coffee cups and sugar and cream containers.

"Just in time." The mill manager stepped forward to take it from her. "Let's fix ourselves a cup of this stuff, Clay, and head out on the grand tour. There're a lot of things I want to show you. When we're finished, you'll have no doubts about the environmental safety of this place."

Clay lurched to his feet far faster than any offer of coffee could have prompted. He was ready for a walkabout, a long walkabout. He needed to move and move fast to combat a feeling like acid eating a hole in his gut. He hadn't felt this disoriented since a drunken cowboy had sucker-punched him in a Calgary bar. Damn it, he should have known she was too good to be true.

At noon, as Clay headed back to the estate, he stopped at the town's only liquor store. He hadn't gotten seriously hammered in years, but tonight was definitely the time to break the trend.

****

Clay woke and, for a moment, lay perfectly still as he tried to orient himself. His mouth felt as if he'd just finished a banquet of cotton wool. When he started to get up, a blinding pain shot through his head somewhere behind his eyes.

"Ah, man!" He grabbed his temples as his stomach roiled. With a groan he stumbled to his feet and into the bathroom.

A half hour later he emerged showered, shaved, and feeling vaguely—just vaguely—as if he might live. He glanced into the crazed mirror above the old dresser beside his bed and groaned. He looked like what his stepfather would have described as a dog's dinner, although he'd never have allowed any dog of his to eat anything that looked like he did. His eyes were bloodshot, and he had bags under his eyes worthy of the worst bum he'd ever seen living in a cardboard box in a city street. And he had that meeting with Madison and her committee in two hours.

"I know, I know." He looked down at Chance staring up at him. "I acted like a fool. Sorry. But I did give you your dinner and water before I got bombed. That should count for something. At least you don't have reason to report me to that two-faced woman from the SPCA."

He turned back to the mirror. *Damn, damn, damn.* How he could have been so stupid as to let a woman

he'd just met make him behave like he had last night...
But, man, oh, man, learning the truth about her had
been a hard punch in the gut. He'd already started
having fantasies about her, for God's sake.

Well, no use regretting or rehashing. Right now he
had to see to the animals and make himself presentable
for that meeting. As he pulled on his jeans and zipped
them up, he spoke to Chance, who sat waiting by the
door.

"Don't worry. I'm not about to let Dr. Madison
Todd turn me into an alcoholic. Or screw me
over...again. Now"—he pulled on his shirt—"let's
head downstairs and outside and hope a few cups of
coffee and some fresh air will work magic on this face
and body. Lucky I brought a suit and white shirt with
me. Maybe I can knock her a bit off center by dressing
like the CEO of Glendon Forest Products."

Chapter Seven

Madison dressed carefully for her first official meeting with Glendon Forest Products' new owner in her position as vice-chair of the Chemsly Citizens' Committee. The beige suit, with its neatly cut jacket and a skirt that revealed just enough leg to be eye-catching, was something she wouldn't normally wear to a town meeting, but she wanted to knock Clay Archer off balance. Confident he didn't yet know she was the main force behind the citizen's committee, she hummed her favorite country tune as she wound her hair up into a knot at the back of her head. She couldn't wait to see his expression when she walked into the hospital boardroom where the meeting was to be held.

But when she leaned into the dresser mirror to apply a light coat of "Barely There" to her lips, the pressure of the slender gold tube brought a memory flooding back. That kiss on the verandah of the old house had been more than a light brush across her mouth. Clay Archer had, in the space of a few seconds, driven her senses wild. Sometime during his years of absence from Chemsly he'd learned to kiss. Oh, my, yes, he certainly had.

Madison let the hand holding the lipstick drop to the dresser and stared into the mirror. *What am I thinking? Didn't Jason Kenny teach me anything about getting involved with tall, dark, handsome men?* She still shriveled inside each time she recalled his words the day she'd suggested he come to Chemsly on their next leave, to meet her family.

"Madison, listen. You've got to understand." He'd stood before her, devastatingly virile and sexy in khaki bush clothes, sleeves rolled up to reveal a deep tan that also darkened his face and neck. "I've got another life back in Canada. There's a girl...a woman. She's administrative director at a prestigious hospital in Vancouver. She's going to get me a good position there. I was seeing her before I came out here…"

Madison hadn't waited to hear any more. She'd whirled and strode back into their tent. She hadn't cried as she'd stuffed clothes into a duffel bag. She couldn't. The pain was a hard, dry knot inside her throat, brutal in its intensity.

He didn't say anything a few minutes later when he ducked inside. He'd glanced over at her, then picked up his medical bag and left.

Madison pulled herself back to the present and raised the lipstick to rub "Barely There" as hard and bright as she could on her lips.

Clayton Archer, you'd better be on your toes today.

****

"Going my way?"

In the hospital parking lot, Madison whirled from locking her SUV and faced Clay Archer. His lips quirked upwards in a smile that didn't extend to the edges of the Ray-Bans he wore. The affable cowboy she'd met three days ago was gone, along with his Stetson and boots. A stranger in an elegant grey business suit, charcoal silk tie, snow-white shirt, and shiny black dress shoes stood in front of her.

He didn't need to tell her. His demeanor said it all. Somehow he'd learned about her involvement with the Chemsly Citizens' Committee.

"Good morning." She pulled her wits together and favored him with what she hoped was an equally wintry smile. "I believe I am."

She hefted her purse and reached down to pick up the briefcase she'd placed on the pavement beside her 4x4. He was quicker.

"Allow me." He snatched it up. "It's probably heavy, full of lots of documentation aimed at closing my mill." Before she could protest, he was striding toward the hospital's main entrance.

Fuming, she followed him, knowing that his simple act was about to ruin her carefully planned, efficient-looking, independent entrance into the boardroom. Short of trying to recover her briefcase and most likely causing a scene in front of the hospital, she had no choice but to accept his unwelcome courtesy. When they reached the building, he paused and held the door for her. Inside, he removed his sunglasses and looked around.

"Hard night?" She couldn't contain the snide remark as she saw his eyes.

"Little bit. Which way?"

She heaved what she hoped sounded like an exasperated sigh and pointed to a large sign with the word "boardroom" in block letters and an arrow pointing left.

"Follow me."

Repressed anger made her voice deeper than normal. She hoped he didn't detect its tremor of outrage. *Don't lose your cool, Dr. Todd, not in front of him.*

He pulled open the boardroom door and held it as she preceded him inside. *The man's insufferable.* Fighting back the urge to kick him in the shins, she faced the group gathered around the long table inside.

Flashing cameras blinded her.

When the spots cleared, she found herself confronted by two people with the paraphernalia of media types. The first she recognized as Bob Brooks, editor and publisher of the town's weekly newspaper. The other person, a young woman in jeans and a bomber jacket, she guessed to be from the provincial daily. They had no doubt caught an image of Clay Archer smiling and carrying her briefcase while she'd looked like something that had just swallowed a sour pill. The description flew across her mind as she took a seat and tried to dismiss the incident from her mind.

It was a small gathering: Dr. Steven McLean; her mother, Molly Todd; Rick Reid; Chrissy Manderson, his secretary; and, to her utter astonishment, seated beside the mill manager, her brother-in-law, Jordan Anderson. The latter glanced up apprehensively at Madison before lowering his gaze to his big, work-hardened hands clasped on the table.

What is Jordan doing here? He's not a member of the committee. What rotten scheme have those two bastards cooked up that involves my brother-in-law? He looks positively ill.

"Clay, Maddy, good to see you." Rick got up from his seat, affable grin in place, hand extended. He shook hands first with Madison (as the cameras clicked again) and then with Clay. "Have a seat, have a seat." He further infuriated Madison by continuing, "Thanks for helpin' Dr. Todd with her material, Mr. Archer, sir," as Clay placed her briefcase on the table in front of her. "Now, let's get right to it, shall we? First, I think introductions are in order." He proceeded to name those around the table, leaving her brother-in-law for last.

"And here we have my special guest, one of Glendon Forest Products' best and most dedicated workers, shift boss Jordan Anderson," he ended. "We'll hear from him a bit later."

He slapped Jordan on a shoulder, grinning down at him. Madison's brother-in-law acknowledged the gesture with a slight flinch, keeping his gaze focused on his hands. His face had a greyish tinge that made him look decidedly ill.

What's happened? Jordan, what threats have they made that have you looking so sick? I swear, if they've done anything to hurt you or my sister's family...

Jordan Anderson wasn't a rich man or a well educated one. He'd gone to work at the mill straight out of high school and worked his way up to shift boss. Marrying chartered accountant Paige Todd seven years later had been the highlight of his life, more than he'd ever dreamed possible, as he hadn't been shy to tell people. When she'd become pregnant with twins and expressed a desire to take a few years off to be a full-time mother, he'd readily agreed. Anything his Princess Paige wanted was his command, even if it had meant taking on heavy overtime to keep up payments on their home and cars and provide Paige and the children with every possible comfort. He didn't deserve to be made to suffer as he obviously was.

"Steve, you goin' to chair this powwow, or will I?" Rick Reid glanced around the room and ended up grinning at the doctor. "Sooner we get started, the sooner we can break for coffee. Chrissy went to a lot of work settin' up a snack for us. Wouldn't want to disappoint her, now, would we?" He waved his arm to indicate a corner table draped with a snow-white cloth and laden with coffee urn, muffins, fruit, and all the necessary complements.

"Probably you should, Rick." Dr. McLean leaned back in his chair. "I could be called away any minute. I have a couple of critically ill patients."

As the small hospital's only surgeon, he had an intense workload. Madison knew he'd taken on the chairperson position of the committee because he knew his name would add credibility to the cause and because he felt that at least some of Madison's claims had validity—even though, as yet, he had no hard laboratory proof. He didn't have the time or energy for the position, and both he and Madison knew it.

Exasperation pricked her. She knew Dr. McLean was tired, she knew he could be summoned to a patient at any moment, but there he was, in front of the media, letting Rick Reid take command of this all-important meeting instead of handing the reins to her as vice-chair of the committee.

Stay calm. Coming across as a wildly agitated female suffering from acute PMS isn't the way to go.

"Okay. It shouldn't be all that difficult." Rick Reid cast one of his appealing grins at the media. "With the press in attendance, I'm sure we'll all be on our best behavior."

That's right, Rick. Give them your best good-ole-boy smile.

"Ready, Dr. Todd?" The mill manager's smile was

as bright and innocent as sunshine.

"Whenever you are." Madison snapped open her briefcase.

"Good, good. Then I'll call this meetin' to order. First off, I'd like to pass around a few handouts for your perusal. Chrissy?"

The secretary picked up a stack of booklets from a corner table and began handing them around the table. Madison stole a glance at Clay Archer and saw he was leaning back in his chair, elbows resting on its arms, fingers steepled.

He caught her glance and kinked his lips into another irritatingly all-knowing smile. She repressed the urge to grind her teeth and turned her attention to the documents Chrissy had placed in front of her. He was in for it now. Without his cowboy getup, he was just another man, and she planned to take him down.

The pages were bound and covered with plastic, with the title "Documentation Relating to Pollution Control at Glendon Forest Products, Chemsly Division" in large and impressive black letters across its front.

"I'll ask you all to take a few minutes to glance through this little novella," Reid said. "It's not *Gone with the Wind*, mind you, but it's mighty fine readin'…at least from this town's point of view."

There was silence except for the rustle of turning pages for the next few minutes as they all scanned the documentation, most with government stamps of approval and official signatures slashed across them certifying that Glendon Forest Products met and in some cases exceeded environmental standards.

At one point Madison felt she was being watched and glanced up to see Clay Archer looking at her, his gaze intense and penetrating. On impulse she narrowed her eyes into a belittling smirk.

A camera flashed.

Chagrined, she returned her attention to the booklet while her mind wrote tomorrow's probable headline: "Clean Environment Committee Vice-Chair Dr. M. Todd glares at Glendon Forest Products' new owner Clay Archer during recent confrontation."

****

"Everyone ready to resume?" Ten minutes later, Rick Reid drew himself up in his chair and glanced around the table. A murmur of consent answered.

"Good. Let's get on with it. Any questions on the documentation?"

"Mr. Chairman?"

"The Chair recognized Dr. Madison Todd. Go ahead, Doctor."

He smiled benevolently over at her, and Madison guessed her blood pressure skyrocketed. Fighting to remain calm and in control, she took several file folders from her briefcase and stood.

"I have handouts, too." *Damn, how come-backish that sounds.* "I'd like to distribute them now, if I may."

"Certainly, Doctor." Rick waved an all-encompassing arm. "Pass them around, by all means. We want everything out in the open, don't we, Clay…er, Mr. Archer?"

Could the man get any more exasperating? She rounded the table, passing out the folders that looked ridiculously skimpy beside Rick Reid's fat analysis.

"While you're doin' that, Doctor, I'm going to take a minute to tell the folks a bit about our guest, Jordan Anderson. As I've said, Jordan is one of our best shift bosses. He's been employed at the mill for nearly twenty years. He's willin' to testify that he's never suffered the loss of a single day's work due to illness."

Madison paused in rounding the table and stared at her brother-in-law. From the corner of her eye she saw the shock she was feeling reflected on her mother's face.

"Well, speak up, Jordan." The mill manager grinned encouragement. "Tell us the good news."

Jordan glanced about the table, pausing an instant when his gaze met Madison's, then rushing on to come to a complete halt before his mother-in-law's astonished expression.

"I…"

"Come on, buddy, out with it," Rick Reid pushed. "We can't fudge around here all mornin'. Our new boss has a statement of his own to make."

"I've never been sick." Jordan dropped his gaze to his hands clenched together on the table, knuckles white. "Nor have any of the guys on my shift…not because of the mill, anyway."

His broad shoulders slumped as he finished speaking, and he kept his eyes downcast.

"Well, then, there now." The mill manager drew a deep, satisfied breath and leaned back in his chair. "That wasn't so bad, was it? You folks from the press got all that, I hope? Good, good. Now, Clay—sorry again, Mr. Archer—has a few words to say before we break for coffee. The floor's yours, Mr. Archer." He swept out an arm in Clay's direction.

Madison saw the new owner hesitate and draw a deep breath. Finally he leaned forward, rested his elbows on the table, laced his fingers together, and spoke.

"You'll have to excuse me if I'm a little slow off the mark," he said. "I didn't receive an agenda for this meeting. I thought we'd be hearing from the Citizens' Committee first and then Mr. Reid and I would have a chance to rebut their concerns. Since that hasn't turned out to be the order of events, I'll be brief and get right to the point. We don't want to keep anyone here all morning, and I'm sure Dr. Todd has a number of concerns she wishes to address once I'm finished."

He leaned back in his chair. "I'm planning on upping the mill's output by twenty percent. My manager and I have already set the wheels in motion toward that goal. It'll mean bigger profits and some nice bonuses for employees."

Madison nearly choked. *Good God, increasing production! More noxious emissions! The man doesn't care about this town at all!*

"Next year," he continued, glancing in her direction, "if all goes well with this expansion, we'll be adding another plant designed to produce paper napkins and towels."

"Hope you media folks got all that." Rick Reid turned to the couple. "The CEO of Glendon Forest Products has spoken. Big things are in store for us here in Chemsly, and it's all thanks to Mr. Clayton Archer. Now." He turned to Madison, the smugness mirrored in his face incensing her. "Dr. Todd, your words, please."

"My words!" Emotions at fever pitch, her response aired in a blast of outrage. "Anything I could say now would be like fighting a forest fire with a squirt gun! But I'm not finished, trust me." She swung on Clay. "I'll find a way to block your expansion and shut you down before any more people get sick. Just watch me!"

She snapped her briefcase shut, turned, and strode out of the room, her heart hammering so violently she wondered that the whole room couldn't hear.

Again the cameras flashed.

****

She was inserting the key into the door of her vehicle when she felt a hand on her arm. Whirling, she faced Clay Archer.

"Can we go somewhere and talk?"

Chapter Eight

"Are you insane?" She faced him, outrage urging her to attack him, to scratch and claw like an enraged feline. "After what you and your buddy Rick Reid did in there? I've heard of playing down and dirty, but what you pulled just now was way below that. Forcing my brother-in-law to testify in front of my mother and me…"

"Jordan Anderson is your brother-in-law?" He had the good grace to look nonplussed.

"Oh, don't play innocent with me." She repressed the urge to swing her briefcase at him. "You and your manager set that up together to throw me off my game. Sorry, but it isn't going to work."

"I didn't know Jordan Anderson is a member of your family, I swear. If I had, I never would have allowed Rick to get him to make that statement."

"Force him to testify, you mean!"

"Whatever. Your mother especially should never have had to face it. Furthermore, I had no idea Rick was inviting the press."

"Do you really expect me to believe you?" Madison glared up into his face and wished all the anger and hatred she was feeling toward him were arrows shooting out of her eyes directly into his.

"Yes." He didn't flinch. "Because I'm not a liar."

Something in his blunt directness told her that was

the truth. The thought made her pause.

"Come out to the house for lunch in an hour," he continued. "We have to talk...alone. No media, no Rick Reid. We've got big issues to resolve, and the sooner we get to it the better. This game of dirty pool can't continue, or it will destroy a lot of innocent people...like your family."

"Oh, come on. If you really cared about my family, you'd close down that killing machine you call a mill. You'd..."

"Come out to the house for lunch in an hour," he interrupted her tirade. "I'll be waiting...alone."

He turned and headed toward his own vehicle. Madison stood staring after him, too astounded by his invitation to move.

When mobility returned, she flung her purse and briefcase into her vehicle and clambered in after them. Seconds later, she whirled across the parking lot to cut Clay Archer off as he drove toward the exit.

Glancing into her rearview mirror, she smirked to see his face hardening as he braked with a dragging of tires.

"Lunch at his place...in an hour!" she scoffed, spinning her little Jeep out onto the street. "Yeah, right! As soon as hell freezes over!"

****

"Mr. Archer?"

Clay looked up from the spinach selections at the Chemsly Food Mart to face Madison's mother.

"Mrs. Todd. Hello." Her friendly smile and greeting startled him after what had happened a half hour earlier in that boardroom.

"You're settling in out at your house?" She

indicated his cart stacked with food and other staples.

"Trying to." He grinned. "I'm a passable cook, but not much good at setting up housekeeping. Look…" He sobered. "I want to apologize for what happened at that meeting earlier. I didn't know Jordan Anderson was a member of your family."

"Thank you for explaining." She favored him with a soft smile. "It wasn't a very nice thing to do."

"You've got that right."

"It must be difficult for you alone out there at your old home." Her expression, softened with concern, made him think how beautiful she was, all gentle and caring. Like Madison might have been before her father's death and she'd taken up the crusade to close his mill. "I'm sure there are memories…"

"Yeah, well, there are those."

"I remember your mother before she became ill. A lovely woman. I regret I didn't visit her after she became housebound, but your stepfather wasn't…"

"Exactly welcoming. I know." Clay looked down into his cart, afraid Molly Todd would see too much emotion in his expression.

"Well, let *me* try to made amends." She laid a hand over his on the chrome handle of his shopping cart. "Come to dinner at our home some evening."

"I thank you for the invitation, but I'm not sure that would be a good idea." Although her invitation startled him, he managed to reply appropriately.

"Because earlier this morning my daughter and I appeared your sworn enemies? Mr. Archer, if anything worthwhile came out of that meeting, it was the fact that scheming and animosity will get us nowhere. We need to cooperate, work together, not back-bite and undermine."

"There's nothing to cooperate about." A sudden need to defend his mill overcame him. Molly Todd's reference to his mother and her miserable life had reinforced his dedication to his goal. "The mill is one hundred percent safe. Your daughter and her committee will just have to accept the fact."

"Oh, dear, dear." Molly shook her head sadly. She brightened as she started to move away. "Nevertheless, the dinner invitation stands. I'll be in touch."

****

"Madison, you have to come out to the estate right now!" Clay Archer's words were a harsh order when she picked up her office telephone three hours later.

"Hold on just one minute, Mr. Archer. I chose not to accept your invitation to lunch, and that's it. Don't think that issuing an ultimatum will…"

"For God's sake! This has nothing to do with lunch or us. Chance has been hit by one of the delivery trucks! He's barely breathing!"

"I'm on my way." Madison dropped the receiver into its cradle and grabbed her black emergency bag. "You'll have to bring Ginger in for her shots tomorrow, Mrs. Mason," she called to the owner of the last patient in her waiting room. "There's an emergency."

Moments later she was on the road and driving at the top of the speed limit toward Clay Archer's farm. She hadn't stopped to wonder if his call might be a ruse. If there was even the vaguest possibility that an animal might be suffering, her duty was to get to it as fast as possible. She also had a deep gut feeling that Clay Archer had been telling the truth when he'd said he wasn't a liar.

****

He was waiting for her on the front verandah and strode down the steps to meet her, looking tense and drawn.

"Thank God!" He pulled open the driver's door. "He's in the parlor. His breathing is shallow."

He took her arm and started to drag her out of the 4x4.

"Wait, wait! Let me get my bag." She stopped him, even as his desperate concern for his dog wiped away a lot of the animosity she'd felt toward him earlier in the day.

"Oh, right." He released her and stepped back. "Sorry."

"It's okay." She picked up her bag. "I understand. Now let's get to the patient."

****

"I'll need x-rays before I can be certain of the full extent of his injuries." She stood and faced Clay Archer after a cursory examination of the dog she'd found lying wrapped in quilts on the parlor floor. "We'll take him to my surgery."

"Sure." He dropped to his knees beside her and reached to gather the dog up into his arms.

"No!" She stopped him. "Not like that. We have to keep him as immobile as possible. Can you find a piece of plywood?"

"Definitely." He leaped to his feet and was off outside in long strides. Madison watched him go, then returned her attention to her patient with renewed hope in her heart. A man who cares as deeply for his dog as Clayton Archer obviously did couldn't be totally indifferent to human suffering.

****

Clay gave up pacing the length and breadth of Madison's outer office and sank into one of the hard, wooden chairs along the wall. He was on his third cup of coffee, and caffeine was making him twitchy and barely able to contain himself. He had to try to relax.

He drew a deep breath and let his gaze roam over the austere room. No frills, just a big, clean, practical space. Dr. Madison apparently had no time for cute puppy pictures or fancy wallpaper. On one wall he recognized a map of the area with certain regions highlighted with a yellow marker, then mostly x'd out. As if she'd been looking for something and then eliminating places. *Hmmm.*

He turned his attention to her desk. It held two framed pictures, their backs to him. Curious, he pulled himself to his feet and went to look at them.

The first one was a photo of Molly Todd, Jordan, a gorgeous woman who looked a lot like a younger version of Molly—probably Jordan's wife—a couple of kids, and the doctor herself. A tall, handsome, middle-aged man with white hair and a smiling face stood between Molly and Madison, an arm about each of them. Madison was looking up at him, her face bright and smiling. Her father, Clay decided, holding the picture up to the light to get a better look. This group was a far cry from what he'd called his family. Their joy in being together shone from the photo. His mouth quirked into a sardonic grimace.

He replaced it on the desk and picked up the second picture. Madison stood beside the same silver-haired man, both of them laughing into the camera. The man was holding a small brown terrier that looked as happy as they did.

An unflattering emotion washed over him, one he never thought he'd feel. It was envy: envy of Madison and her family.

****

"How is he?" He bolted from the chair. It was nearly eight p.m. as Madison emerged from her operating room and faced him. A collection of cardboard coffee cups in her garbage can indicated how he'd passed the time.

"Stable," she replied, pulling off her white smock. She saw him flinch as his gaze fell on the bloodstains smeared across its front. "It'll be morning before I can tell you with certainty he's going to make it."

"Ah, man!" He turned and strode across the room to stare out the front window into the autumn dusk of the deserted street.

He put his hands on his hips, legs planted apart. In well-fitted jeans and a faded blue plaid shirt, he was rugged, handsome, virile, the cowboy again...yet now somehow vulnerable and alone. Completely alone. He had no family and no friends that she knew of in the area.

She stifled the urge to go to him, to put a comforting hand on his arm as she would have with other patient owners. Yet she couldn't risk any more physical contact with the man. Not if she wanted to maintain a detached impartiality, not if she wanted to retain the full force of her antagonism toward him and his mill.

"I'll stay with him tonight," she said. "He'll need watching. I'd appreciate it if you'd go next door and get me a sandwich and coffee. I see you know the way."

When he turned to face her, she inclined her head toward the empty cups and smiled.

"Yeah, well." He let a sheepish grin creep over his features. "I was a little stressed."

"I understand." She couldn't help it. She spoke gently, from the heart.

"Thanks." Their gazes met. Something she hadn't felt since Dr. Jason Kenny coursed through her veins. Only this time it was stronger and different in a way she couldn't label.

"Turkey, roast beef, ham?" He headed for the door.

"Turkey with tomatoes and lettuce and lots of mayo." She snapped out of it and gave her order. "And one very large coffee, black."

****

He was back within ten minutes. Madison had used the time to put on a clean top, splash cold water on her face, free her hair from her operating cap, and give it a quick brush so it fell down around her shoulders. Revived, she sat behind her desk filling out a report on Chance.

He stopped just inside the doorway, cardboard cup and brown paper sack in hand, and stared.

"What?" she asked glancing up.

"I've never seen you with your hair like that," he said. "Nice, very nice."

"Thanks, but I think all that caffeine may be getting to you." She managed to control the light thrill of pleasure his words had given her. "May I have my supper, please? I'm famished. You should head back to the estate. You have other animals that need care."

"Damn it, you're right." He moved to her desk and placed the take-out order in front of her. "Okay, I'll feed and water them and come right back."

"No, you won't." She reached for the food and began to remove it from the bag. He'd bought her a container of hot vegetable soup and a biscuit, as well as the coffee and sandwich. It looked wonderful. It had been a long day, with only an apple for lunch. "They'll need tending first thing in the morning, as well. Furthermore, I've only got one cot here."

"I can sleep on the floor, or in a chair." His words were coming out fast, jerky. Too much caffeine. Madison knew the symptoms.

"No, I'll call you if there's any change." She finished spreading her meal out in front of her. "Go, please."

"Okay, okay, but can I see him before I go…just for a minute?" The sincere appeal in those wonderful blue eyes was undeniable.

"All right, but just for a minute. He's heavily sedated and on an IV. I don't want him disturbed."

"Thanks." The word came out hoarse with emotion. "Chance has been with me day and night for the past five years. I don't know what I'll do if…"

This time she didn't stop herself. She reached out and placed a comforting hand on his arm. "I'll do my best."

"I know you will." Again their gazes met; again Madison felt the wild, nebulous something she couldn't explain. But it was only for a second, before he moved past her toward the surgery.

****

Clay snapped the tab on the beer can and dropped into a threadbare wing chair in his shabby parlor. This was his home, yet he had no fond memories of it aside from his mother's attempts to show him affection in the face of opposition from her husband. The man had insisted on treating Clay as a nuisance, something to be sent off to boarding schools with as much concern as a person might brush a fly from his shoulder.

Drained, dead tired, too keyed up to sleep, his mind kept racing back to that moment in the dooryard hours earlier. The crash, Chance's scream, the driver's shouts.

He remembered bolting outside. The image of the dog's pain-crazed thrashing in the dust before he lapsed into unconsciousness made him flinch. He took a long pull on his beer and stretched out with a deep sigh. Chance had to be okay. Damn it, the little critter was all he had.

He remembered Madison—the blood on her smock, the exhaustion mirrored in her face after three hours in her surgery. He felt a shiver run through him. She'd fought for Chance's life with every ounce of her strength and knowledge.

Quite a lady. Damn shame she's turned out to be my enemy.

He stopped himself right there as other thoughts of Madison Todd began to invade his mind. Thoughts he couldn't afford to have. Not now. Not under the present circumstances. The mill expansion had to be all-important if he planned to have the Abby Archer Memorial Rehab Center up and running within the year. He couldn't get involved with someone who could derail the entire project.

He stood and ambled over to the window to stare out into the darkness. The moon was rising, white and stark, over the black night forest. It had been another hot, rainless day. Each one, he knew, made the bush more tinder dry, more vulnerable to the slightest spark. If those trees went up in flames, so would his plans for the profits from his mill. With nothing to process, the place would be useless.

He returned to his chair, polished off his beer, and leaned back, willing himself to relax. He'd tended the horses as soon as he came home, but he hadn't made a meal for himself. He knew he should eat something, take a shower, and go to bed. But he couldn't. Instead he headed back to the refrigerator for a second beer.

Chapter Nine

He awoke the next morning, head thrown back, mouth feeling as if it were lined with cotton wool. *Damn it, snoring again.* Blinking, he grimaced as he slowly righted himself and got out of the chair. He must have fallen asleep in the parlor after one can of beer and a mouthful out of a second. Man, he must really have been wiped out.

Chance. Had he made it through the night? He glanced toward the newly installed telephone on an end table by the door. The message light wasn't flashing. Madison hadn't called. That was good, meant things were probably stable at the clinic. Or, hopefully, better.

Trying to expel some of the stiffness from his joints and muscles, he stretched and glanced at his watch. Seven thirty a.m. He'd better get moving. He had to tend the horses and feed the cat before he headed back into town.

****

He arrived at her clinic an hour later. Only when he stepped inside and caught the expression on the face of the elderly woman who was Madison's first client of the day did he realize how he must look. Unshaven and wearing the same clothes from the previous day, he must present a pretty rough image. He'd paused only long enough to splash cold water from the barn pump over his face before jumping into his truck and heading for town.

"He'll be fine, Mrs. Dobson." Madison, looking rested and squeaky clean in fresh jeans and sweatshirt, stepped out of the surgery and handed a cat carrier to the elderly woman. "Casper just needed a couple of stitches. I'd advise you to keep him indoors at night…at least until he's completely healed. He is a tom, you know."

"Thank you, dear." The woman peered into the cage. "Naughty boy. I hope you behaved for Maddy." She turned her attention back to the vet, who was watching, a smile on her face. "I'll pay you on Thursday, when I get my Social Security check, Maddy, if that's okay."

"Actually it was such a small job it's not worth my making out a bill." She shrugged. "But if you insist on paying, I wouldn't object to one of your state-of-the-art apple pies."

"No problem at all." Relief filled the woman's face. "I'll bring you one tomorrow, in time for lunch." She leaned close to Madison. "Do you want me to stay while you deal with this fellow, dear?" She cast her eyes meaningfully over Clay.

Man, I must look bad.

"That won't be necessary, Mrs. Dobson." Madison gently escorted her to the door. "I know him. I'll see you tomorrow."

Once the door had closed behind the woman and her cat, Madison turned to Clay.

"Have you eaten or slept since you left here yesterday?"

"Slept. Sorry if I alarmed your clientele. How's Chance?"

"Come and see." She held open the door of the surgery and indicated he was to precede her inside.

Chance lay on a large, overstuffed dog bed beneath a window, a heavy sheath of bandages around his middle. Beside him lay Ceilidh, eyes round and alert. The room also held a narrow cot, a small dresser, and a door leading to a modest bathroom. Clay barely noticed. He was too busy dropping to his knees beside his dog.

Chance stirred and, as recognition brightened his eyes, tried to struggle into an upright position.

"Take it easy, pal." Clay stopped him with a hand on his shoulder. "Stay. No need to get up."

At his friend's words, Chance stopped wriggling and lay still except for a weak tail wag he couldn't contain.

For a few moments Clay rubbed the dog's head gently. Relief had taken away words. Finally he turned to Madison.

"How is he?"

"Not great, but without any complications he should make it."

"Thank God!" Avoiding her eyes, he spoke hoarsely. "And thank you, Dr. Todd."

"My job," she said, but he caught a touch of emotion in her voice that said she was pleased, too.

The front door opened. "We're back here, Mom," she called. "I asked my mother to sit with Chance while I get some breakfast and run a few errands," she explained when he looked puzzled by her response to someone she couldn't see. "She's a registered nurse."

A moment later Molly Todd, looking relaxed and youthful in jeans and a plaid cotton shirt, came to stand beside her daughter and smile down at the man and his dog.

"Good morning, Mr. Archer. Madison tells me it looks as if your friend is going to be just fine. I'm glad."

"Thank you." He stood, feeling knee high to a snake. After the way his mill manager had treated her family at the previous day's meeting, he found it difficult to face her continuing kindness. Her invitation to dinner later, in the supermarket, hadn't helped his sense of shame and chagrin. "Your daughter's dedication and skill pulled him through."

"Maddy is a wonderful vet," Molly agreed, smiling fondly at her younger child. "I'm very proud of her."

"Mom, did you come here to take over for a while or just to be unbearably saccharine?" Madison gave her mother a quick hug.

"Both," she said, kneeling beside Chance. "Are there any special instructions?"

"Just watch him closely, and if you see any negative change, call my cell." To Clay, she said, "Come on. Chance needs to rest."

****

Outside he kept pace with her as she turned the corner to the side of the building and into the small parking lot where her Jeep and his truck waited side by side.

"How long will your mother be on duty?" he asked.

"Until noon. It's Saturday, so I don't have a patient list. If it weren't for Chance, the office would be closed today. Don't worry. I'll be back before Mom has to leave. Chance won't be left unattended."

107

"I knew he wouldn't be. I was wondering if you had time to have breakfast with me, my treat. I noticed the restaurant down the street has a great-looking special advertised in the window."

"I don't think that our being seen together in what could look like a congenial get-together would be a good idea," she said. "I haven't changed my position on your mill, and I want people to know it. I still plan to fight you tooth and nail to prevent its continuing in its present state. And as for upping production and expanding…"

"So what you're saying is that this has been a temporary truce forced on you by Chance's accident?"

"That's it."

She turned to get into her vehicle, but he stopped her with a hand on her arm.

"Okay. I understand. That being said, I think it's time you checked on the horses again. So how about coming out to the estate while your mother's on duty? I'll fix breakfast for us."

"Well…" She hesitated. "Okay. I do need to submit a report on their progress to the SPCA this week. I have to make a couple of stops first. I'll follow you out shortly."

Maybe it's time to pour on a little more honey and see what happens.

****

He came downstairs freshly shaved and showered, in clean shirt and jeans, to the smell of freshly brewed coffee. In the kitchen he found Madison putting the finishing touches on the table. It was neatly set for two, with a small vase of fresh flowers and a basket of muffins in its center. Auburn hair pulled back into a ponytail with just enough curls escaping to frame her face, she turned and smiled at him as he came into the room.

Damn it, she's the prettiest thing I've ever seen.

Warning bells went off in his head. He suddenly recalled his stepfather's words: "If it looks too good to be true, it probably is." *Quite possibly the only helpful words the old bastard ever bothered to address to me. They're coming in handy now.*

"I let myself in while you were upstairs. Sit. Please." She indicated a chair at the table and smiled. She opened the oven of the gleaming new electric range and removed two plates. Each held a golden-topped mini quiche.

"I didn't hear your SUV." He found his voice over his surprise. "Must have been in the shower. I didn't expect this." He spread out his hands to indicate the table. "My plan only went as far as scrambled eggs and bacon."

Amazed and growing more apprehensive by the second, he took his place at the table. She put one plate at each setting, then served coffee and orange juice.

"Dig in." She sat down opposite him and smiled. Again.

Those damned warning bells are all-out clanging now.

"Looks great." He stirred his coffee, trying to shake the feeling an ax was about to fall. "You must have done some fast shopping on the way out here."

"There's a convenience store along the way, owned by a lady I know who makes these great muffins and quiche. She also sells fresh flowers." She cut into her pastry.

"But why? After yesterday…"

"That's exactly why. After Chance's accident yesterday, and the stress you've suffered, I thought you deserved a little TLC, no matter how despicably you and Rick Reid behaved. Anyway"—her tone lightened—"it's been a long time since I've had anyone to share a real breakfast with."

"Yeah?" He found himself following up too quickly, too intensely on the remark. "When was that?"

"A long time ago." She was trying to sound nonchalant, but he glimpsed the hurt in her eyes before she switched the subject. "How are the horses?"

"Fine, I think. I'll let you be the judge after we eat." He turned his attention to the food, but images of Madison being domestic with Tom Mills had begun to muck up his mind. It had to have been Tom Mills.

The sound of a vehicle coming up the drive distracted him, and he glanced out the window to see the farrier's truck.

Perfect timing. Exactly the man I don't want to see just now.

"Seems we have a visitor," he said needlessly. Madison was also looking out the window.

"Tommy," she said simply.

"Yeah…Tommy." God, he hated their having nicknames for each other.

He answered the door when Tom knocked a few moments later.

"Tom. Come in. We're having breakfast. Join us." He tried to be gracious but saw his visitor's face harden at the sight of Madison seated at the table.

"I was passing and thought I'd check on Scout…see how that hoof is doing," Tom said, his gaze on Madison. "Hi, Maddy."

"Good morning, Tommy." Madison stood and headed for the percolator, coffee cup in hand. "Have you eaten? We have muffins left."

Fighting to sound casual. Can't be easy when the guy she used to play house with has stepped in on her having breakfast with someone else. Wonder who called it quits? Or why. Or when. Last year, last month, last week? What does Madison Todd consider a long time? Does she measure it in dog years? Oh, man, I'm getting crazy now.

"No…thanks." Tom stood inside the back door on a threadbare mat. "I'll go on down to the barn. I've got a busy morning. See you later." He grabbed the doorknob behind his back, turned, and was outside in a single, long stride.

Silence. A clock ticked. Finally Madison returned to the table. "Let's finish our breakfast. With luck, we can catch up with Tommy before he leaves. I want to check Scout's hoof while he's still here."

"Okay, sure." He went back to the table and sat down opposite her. He finished off his orange juice, then asked, "Was he the one?"

"Was who what?" She glanced over at him, green eyes innocently wide.

"Oh, come on! You know perfectly well what I mean. Was Tom Mills the guy you used to play house with?"

"What!" She jumped to her feet, making the dishes rattle and the coffee in her freshly filled cup slosh over the rim.

"You heard me." He looked up at her and felt crazy, unreasonable anger twisting his gut.

111

"What makes you think you have any right to that information?" Her eyes flashed emerald fire.

"Damn it, woman!" He scrambled to his feet, rounded the table, and was kissing her, kissing her with the hottest desire he'd ever experienced, before he knew what he was doing.

She responded naturally, reactively, passionately. He let go of reality to immerse himself in the wild joy of it all. His body reacted, his entire being submerged in her unabashed sensuality. She smelled wonderful, felt fantastic, and tasted ever better. He knew what he wanted to do with the rest of the day, rest of the week...

As quickly as it had begun, it was over. She wrenched away, lurching back against the table, scrubbing a hand over her mouth.

"What do you think you're doing?" She glared up at him.

"Damned if I know...again." He struggled to get himself back to behaving rationally. He sat down and picked up a muffin. "I'll let you explain."

"Argh!" With an exasperated snarl she whirled and strode out the back door.

****

As Madison headed toward the barn she struggled to get her heart rate back to normal. She couldn't let Tommy see her like this. She was afraid she was as flushed as a teenager after her first kiss. And her lips. Did they look freshly kissed? Stopping at her Jeep, she took out her black vet bag. Maybe carrying it would make her look more as if she were here on a strictly professional call.

But definitely no more honey where Clay Archer is concerned. It's too downright dangerous.

Those kisses never should have happened. She had to keep a safe distance between that man and herself. She wasn't about to sell out the people of Chemsly for a cowboy's killer good looks, old-fashioned charm, and incredible lovemaking.

Anyway, she knew his type. Dr. Jason Kenny had been an advanced course in what to expect—and not expect—from a handsome, sexy man.

"Hi, Tommy." She stepped into the barn to see the farrier coming out of Scout's box stall. "How's the hoof?"

He closed the door behind him before he turned to face her. "Fine. How's Mr. Glendon Forest Products?" His words, tainted with innuendo, trembled with pent-up anger.

"Tommy, it's not what you think. I came out here this morning…"

"From where? Both of you from your place? Come on, Maddy. I thought you had more common sense. The whole town will be saying you sold out to a pair of blue eyes and a set of broad shoulders!"

He headed toward her, and she saw he was intending to brush past her and leave. She reached out and caught his arm.

"Tommy, you've got to believe me. There's nothing except mill business between us. And the fact that I'm treating his injured dog and malnourished horses."

"Yeah?" He looked down at her, his expression bitter. "It's hard to believe a business discussion made your lips look like that!"

With a shrug he freed himself from her hand, strode out of the barn, and jumped into his pickup.

113

Gunning the motor, he sped off in a cloud of dust.

****

She was examining the mare when Clay Archer appeared in the doorway of the box stall.

"Everything okay?" he asked, leaning against the wall and crossing his arms on his chest. "I saw our farrier hightailing it past the house. Not upset about something, was he?"

"Just in a hurry to get to his next client. He's a busy man."

"Good, fine, then. How's Candy doing?"

"Very good." She moved around the mare to face him. "You've done an excellent job. I'll inform the SPCA."

"Appreciate it."

As she started past him, he moved to block her way. She looked up at him, virile and close and overwhelmingly masculine. Her entire body reacted.

"Madison, we've got to talk, really talk," he said softly, his tone deep and sensuous. "There's something happening between us…something that might be really good if we give it a chance."

"Don't talk crazy!" From somewhere she found the strength to spit the words at him. "There's one huge, filthy pulp-and-paper mill standing right between us, and it always will be…until you come to your senses and do something about it! Now get out of my way. I'll send you my bill."

****

Okay, so he'd behaved like an idiot—worse, a jealous idiot—over a woman he'd kissed twice. Dr. Madison Todd, his sworn enemy, made him behave like a horny sixteen-year-old in the throes of his first crush.

He drove his pitchfork into the sawdust behind Scout and hefted a load of manure out into the wheelbarrow in the stable's corridor with excessive force. *No more letting the woman tease and torment me. All over in that department.*

He threw the fork against the wall and pushed the cart out to the manure pile behind the barn with long, determined strides. *No more waking up in a sweat of need and desire. No more fantasies about fixing up the house and estate with her.* As he flipped the load of sawdust and droppings into the refuse heap, he vowed Dr. Madison Todd would never again play him for a fool.

He had to get over it, find some way to get her out of his head. He propped the wheelbarrow up against the barn and went back inside to pick up the old guitar he'd left in a corner. His security blanket. The thing he'd clung to as a teenager when his stepfather had been particularly harsh and Clay had retreated to the safety of the barn. He'd found it in a back stall, where he'd left it years ago. His thoughts slid back to those days.

There'd been a couple of fancy horses in residence, Glendon Gregory's one self-indulgence. Clay had never been allowed to ride them or even take part in their care. A stable hand had done that type of work. His only friend had been the big grey cat he'd rescued from a ditch near the estate after it had been struck by a vehicle. He'd smuggled it home, filched food for it from the house, and nursed it back to health. She'd been pregnant at the time, and he'd kept her and her litter secretly in the barn until he'd been able to find homes for them.

He sat down on an old bench along one wall and

115

ran his fingers over the guitar stings.

A meow accompanied the notes, and he looked up to see the present resident cat, heavy with pregnancy, sitting a few feet in front of him. As she slowly got to her paws and ambled toward him, he worked his fingers absently over the strings, his heartbeat upping. When she brushed against his leg and finally settled herself against it, he discovered he was smiling, a *déjà vu* sense of comfort washing over him.

He'd been patient, and she had come to him. Maybe if he was patient, if he waited until all this mess about the mill was cleared away, Madison Todd might do the same.

But he'd lured the cat with food and water. The only lure he had that would attract the doctor was the closure of his mill, and that would only happen when hell froze.

Resigned to conditions as they stood, he began to pick a country song and vocalize along with the music.

****

Madison was nearly back to town when she realized she'd forgotten her black bag in the barn.

So much for my dramatic exit.

Swinging her vehicle around, she headed back to the estate. She stopped at the house and got out, deciding to walk down to the barn. The yard had seen a lot of vehicle traffic recently and was becoming rutted. No need to make it worse.

Halfway there, she heard music and paused. The sound of a guitar and a man's voice singing the gentle lilt of her favorite country song floated out into the soft morning air.

"She isn't just another woman…"

Clay? I had no idea he could play and sing. Is he singing about me? Oh, God, Madison, don't be ridiculous. Of course he isn't.

Nevertheless, she paused to listen to the familiar words. They told the story of a woman who'd gotten into the singer's soul.

She waited until the song ended before walking into the barn.

"Forgot my bag." She tried to sound brisk and businesslike as she snatched it up and struggled to ignore the Stetson he was wearing, the boots, the superfitted jeans...

The cat that had been leaning against his leg scurried into hiding.

"Oh, yeah, right." He got up from the overturned bucket on which he'd been sitting and laid the guitar aside.

"I had no idea you were a musician." Her words came out softer, more full of interest than she intended.

"Yeah, well, strictly amateur and self-taught." He picked up the manure fork and headed into Candy's stall. "See you around."

"Yes, see you." Feeling deflated and rejected, Madison turned and walked out of the barn. Annoyance flooded back as she got into her Jeep.

How could I have allowed myself to be so weak, so stupid...to let a not-ugly man wearing a stupid cowboy hat and singing my favorite country song soften me like that? Get real! You're at war with Clay Archer, and you'd better damn well remember it.

Chapter Ten

The following Monday, Madison received two discouraging letters. One was from the provincial government stating that the mill had passed all environmental standards, that there were no apparent reasons for her concerns. The second had come from a toxicologist who declared, given her evidence and that provided by Dr. Steven McLean, he could find no definite proof that pollution from the mill was responsible for any of the local illnesses. There were hints, of course, but without an actual sample from those mysterious holding ponds she'd mentioned there was little more that could be done. Disgusted and discouraged, she threw both letters aside and sat down at her desk to think.

It had been more than a week since her encounter with Clay and Tom at the farm. During that time, she'd conscientiously avoided seeing either of them alone.

Tom had been easy to avoid. He'd apparently decided to stay away from her on his own. Clay, too, had been reticent to be with her. The only time she'd seen him was when he'd come to visit his dog.

She'd been absolutely professional when he visited Chance. The day he took the little dog home, she gave him detailed instructions on Chance's care and handed him a bill for her services, careful to keep a good arm's length distance from him at all times.

That hadn't been difficult. He'd made no move that would suggest he wanted to resume the intimacy of the previous week.

Although she knew she should have been satisfied, even pleased by his behavior, she wasn't. She'd wanted him to show her that kiss had meant something to him, had done to him a bit of what it had done to her. A woman wanted to feel she'd left at least a bit of an impression, even if she wasn't interested in pursuing the relationship.

But he'd only been polite and courteous. He'd paid her bill and driven away with his dog as if he were nothing more than another client.

Stop brooding about the man. You have to get back on track. The mill. Pollution. Sick people. Her thoughts hiccupped. *Dad.*

She drew a deep breath and forced herself to focus on the problem at hand. Apparently there was only one way she would ever prove her case. She had to find the source of the toxic stuff that was contaminating the town, giving the people of Chemsly everything from stomach trouble to cancer. Her thoughts returned to her father.

He'd been convinced that, somewhere in the area, Glendon Forest Products was dumping poisonous waste into unlined containment ponds. But where? The town was ringed with forest, acres and acres of forest. Those ponds could be anything from long, narrow ditches hidden in its depths to crooked trenches masquerading as silty brooks.

She went to a map of the area, kept tacked to her office wall. She often consulted it in order to find some of her more rural clients.

Think, think. There has to be a logical place, somewhere so remote and unattractive even the ardent ATVers, of which Chemsly has a goodly number, don't go. She paused, chewing on her lower lip.

Maybe she should start looking at the problem the other way around. Maybe she should begin by marking off all the forested areas popular for outdoor activities and then investigate what was left.

She took a red pen from her pocket and drew a big circle around an area about twenty miles from town. That was one area she could eliminate. A former military firing range, the region had been closed to the public for years because of the danger of unexploded shells.

"Dr. Todd, Dr. Todd! Misty's awful sick! You've got to help her! Please don't let her die!" Twelve-year-old Jenny Watson burst through the front door, a small grey kitten in her arms.

All thoughts of toxic waste sites vanished as Madison took the limp cat from the little girl.

****

Bone tired, Madison headed home from Jenny Watson's place. In spite of her best efforts, the kitten had died, poisoned by some toxin she hadn't yet identified. After she'd driven the bereft girl home, she'd waited until Mrs. Watson had arrived from work, so Jenny wouldn't be alone with her sorrow. She also wanted to ask the mother, out of the child's hearing, for permission to perform an autopsy on the little animal. It might provide some clue to the toxins being released into the area by the mill.

Mrs. Watson had consented. Her husband, a former mill worker, was in the hospital, his lungs severely damaged.

She was considering all the symptoms and signs she would be looking for in her examination when a horn blasted behind her. Glancing into the rearview mirror, she saw Clay Archer in his pickup, emergency lights flashing, honking for her to stop.

Just what she needed after a trying day. But he'd never played false with her. She believed she knew him well enough to be confident he wouldn't stop her needlessly.

She put on her signal light and pulled over. By the time she'd shifted into park, he was at her door.

"It's Scout," he said without preamble. "I jumped him over a fallen log. He stumbled, and pulled up lame. Can you come?"

"Of course."

****

Twenty minutes later, Madison stood after examining Scout's pastern. "Nothing a good night's rest and some cold compresses won't set right. But I wouldn't try jumping him again without first giving him some training. He's a quarter horse, not a steeplechaser." Madison bent and snapped her black bag shut. "I doubt either of these horses has ever done anything more physically challenging than a quarter-mile gallop on a leisurely trail ride. Have you, boy?"

She straightened up to pat Scout's neck. The gelding snorted.

"I guess I owe him an apology." Clay scratched the animal under the forelock. "He's been out of shape, as well, half starved on over-grazed pasture. I'll take it easier on him."

"Good. How's Chance? Do you want me to take a

look at him before I leave?"

"He appears to be doing fine, but I'd appreciate it if you'd examine him, to be sure."

"I will. Now I have a question. That barn cat...did she have her kittens yet?"

"As a matter of fact, sometime last night. Mother and babies are doing well, but if you'd like to check on them, I'd be grateful." He indicated a box stall to their left.

Inside, Madison found the cat and her family ensconced in a huge, obviously new wicker laundry basket cushioned with an also obviously new quilt. The stainless steel bowls, one filled with water, the other with cat food, sat close beside it. Madison squatted beside the small group and put a careful hand on the mother's head. A soft purr answered her actions, and she looked up at Clay, who'd followed her inside.

"A little elaborate for a barn cat, isn't it?" she asked.

"She deserves pampering." He shrugged and grinned sheepishly. "Being a single parent and all. Do I meet SPCA standards?"

"Definitely. Do you have plans for them?"

"I thought I'd keep 'em, seeing as how there's only four. I need a few good cats around here, judging from the evidence of mice everywhere. I'll have them neutered and spayed, naturally. Don't want to overload the local cat population."

"That little grey one. May I buy her from you?"

"You want the kitten? She's yours. With all you've done for the horses and Chance, I owe you a lot more."

"Actually"—Madison stood and faced him—"she's for a client whose kitten died today. A twelve-year-old girl."

"Then the kitten's definitely yours to give. Losing a pet can be pretty darn traumatic, especially for a kid. What happened?"

"Poisoned." She looked at him evenly. "I'm going to perform an autopsy."

"You're not going to start something else, are you? Now my mill's poisoning children's pets?" His expression hardened. "Haven't you read the documentation Rick handed out at the meeting? Don't you trust government inspectors? Provincial toxicologists?"

"I'm convinced your mill made some pretty hefty campaign contributions during the last elections," she countered.

"Are you saying my company *bought* politicians? That's a serious charge, Dr. Todd."

"Well, the Minister for the Environment is from this riding, isn't he?" She had her hands on her hips, leaning toward him, feeling adrenaline rushing through every artery in her body. This was what she'd been spoiling for, a knock-down, drag-out, gloves-off, no-holds-barred, head-on confrontation with the man whose family's neglect and unconcern had killed her father. "If I were you, I'd take a good hard look at your company accounts and see whose bread Glendon Forest Products has been buttering!"

Before he could reply, she whirled and strode out of the barn.

"I'll check on Chance before I leave," she threw back over her shoulder. "He's not to blame for any of this!"

****

Gail MacMillan

Clay Archer pulled back his boot and kicked the hay bale by the barn door as hard as he could. *Damn the woman, damn her, damn her! She has to be the most exasperating female on the planet.*

He kicked the hay again. And again. It didn't help. The knot of anger still formed a big, hard lump in his gut. With a breathed expletive he turned back to barn work.

Scraping up manure and filling mangers did little to relieve his irritation. Later, as he crossed the yard toward the house, thunder muttered in the distance. Glancing up, he noticed the sky had darkened to an ugly shade of charcoal. Another half-assed storm that probably wouldn't produce a single drop of rain. Like Dr. Todd, all it could possibly do was increase the danger of an all-out disaster for him and his mill.

****

As he arrived at the house, she stepped out of the back door. Looking up at her on the porch, he paused. *Pretty, pretty, pretty. And she tumbles out of bed looking just as terrific. She surely did the morning after the night she spent here at the estate with me, anyway.*

"Chance is doing fine," she said, brushing a stray length of curling hair from her forehead. "But try to keep him quiet for a couple more days."

"I'll do my best, but you know Border Collies." A little grin tugged up the corners of his mouth. "Not a breed that likes to lie around."

"Definitely." That grin hadn't helped. She remained cool and professional. It hurt. He didn't want it this way…not with Madison, no matter what she was trying to do to his mill. "But please make an effort."

She came down the steps, black bag in hand, and

strode past him to her SUV. Seconds later, as he watched her drive away, his gut felt as empty as if he hadn't eaten for a couple of days.

****

"Jenny Watson is asking to see the kitten you promised her." Madison's voice on the telephone two days later took him by surprise. He hadn't expected to hear from her again after their heated exchange, unless it was in a professional capacity regarding the animals. "If you're agreeable, I'll drive her out to the estate in about a half hour. She just wants to visit. I've explained it's far too soon to take it from its mother."

"Sure, fine, okay." He tried to hide his pleasure at the prospect of seeing her again. "Can you bring some of those catalogues and magazines about Victorian home restoration you mentioned? I'm hoping to start work out here shortly."

"Certainly. In fact, you can keep them. I won't be needing them at any time in the foreseeable future."

Ouch! Sucker punch right in his aspirations... again.

"Thanks. See you shortly."

He snapped his cell shut, shoved it into his pocket, and started out of the barn toward the house. Intending to clean up after he'd done the barn work, he'd pulled on yesterday's shirt and jeans when he climbed out of bed that morning, but time had slipped away from him. He needed a shave, a shower, and fresh clothes before she arrived.

Halfway to the house he stopped so abruptly that Chance, who'd been trotting at his heels, ran into the backs of his knees.

"Sorry, buddy." He rubbed the stubble on his chin.

"On second thought, maybe I'll just make coffee. Sprucing myself up for her isn't a good idea. I don't want to look like a teenager on his first date. Play it cool, eh, boy? I'd advise you to do the same with Ceilidh. If you don't mind my saying so, you've been acting way too obvious lately. Now, let's go. We can at least have fresh perked brew and a bowl of cold water for our ladies when they arrive. I've got juice, soda, and milk…the kid should like one of those."

Chance gave a bark and trotted along beside him as he jogged the rest of the way to the house.

****

Madison glanced over at the eager expression on Jenny's face and let a smile curl her lips. A half hour earlier she wouldn't have believed she'd be paying a nonprofessional visit to the Gregory estate. She definitely wouldn't have been looking forward to it. But the girl's enthusiasm to see her new pet had proven contagious, and she'd been caught up in Jenny's anticipation.

Come on, be honest, an annoying little voice in her head mocked. *Admit it. You're looking forward to seeing that blue-eyed, great-bodied cowboy again.*

"Have you decided what you're going to name your kitten?" In an effort to distract herself, Madison glanced over at Jenny and smiled.

The child hesitated and looked out a side window.

"Come on, tell me."

"I was thinking…Maddy—if you don't mind. I heard Mr. Mills, my riding teacher, call you Maddy, and I thought it was cute, and since you got her for me…" A blush suffused her face.

"I'd be honored to have her named for me." A

126

lump of emotion filled her throat. "Thank you, Jenny. I hope Maddy makes you very happy and lives a long, long time."

"She will. If the mill doesn't poison her like it did Misty and our dads." The sudden bitterness in the child's voice startled Madison. For a moment it took her attention from her driving.

"We can't prove it...yet, Jenny," she said gently. "So until we can, we should probably cool it in the accusation department. Remember who's giving you the kitten, okay?"

She hesitated, then nodded. "If you say so, Dr. Todd."

That sounded as if I were defending Clayton Archer. I'd better watch it, or people will think I'm switching sides.

****

Clay was riding Candy in the paddock beside the barn when they arrived at the estate. Involved in a training exercise, he waved to them as he kept the mare at a smooth lope around the perimeter of the field.

"Wow! He can really ride!" Jenny climbed to the top rail of the fence and gazed at the horse and rider, eyes wide.

"Not too shabby," Madison had to admit as she watched man and horse move in near perfect harmony. "You've been taking lessons from Mr. Mills?"

"Yeah, sure, but no way am I as good as that." She continued to stare at Clay and Candy.

He cantered over to the fence and touched his Stetson as he drew rein in front of them.

Damn, but he's handsome on that horse, in that hat, in those jeans, in those boots... Madison halted her involuntary thoughts as he stopped the horse. *Stupid, stupid, Dr. Todd.*

"Welcome, ladies. Glad you could come."

"You ride really well." Admiration shone from Jenny's face and eyes. *Were her heroes cowboys, too?* "I'm taking lessons from Mr. Mills, but no way can I ride like you."

"Tom Mills is a fine horseman." He smiled down at the child. "He'll have you riding better than me in no time. You're Jenny, I guess, and you've come to see your kitten?"

She nodded.

"She's in the barn, in the basket with her mother. Just go slow. Mamma cat is a tad protective."

"No problem. I'll respect her territory." She jumped down from the fence.

"And Jenny?" He stopped her as she started toward the barn. "Would you like to take Candy here for a couple of circuits of the pasture after you've visited with your kitten?"

"Really?" She whirled to face him, enthralled enthusiasm mirrored in words and expression. "That would be great. Thanks, Mr. Archer. I'll go see Maddy and come right back."

"Maddy?" As she ran into the barn, Clay turned to Madison, a grin twitching his lips.

"Her way of thanking me." She stuck her hands into the pockets of her jeans and focused on her running shoes.

"And using Tom Mills' pet name." As she glanced up she saw the grin slide away. "She must hear it a lot, seeing as how she's taking lessons from him."

"Probably." A wicked urge to spur what she

thought could be jealousy and frustration washed over her.

"How about coffee?" With Candy secured to the fence, he left the paddock and banged the gate shut behind him.

"Sure, may as well. Jenny will likely be with Maddy for a few minutes, getting acquainted." She sensed she was irritating him to the bone, and she was enjoying it. "By the way, you looked really hot on that mare. If you weren't the totally uncaring bastard who owns a deadly source of pollution, I might get really turned on."

"Now there's a double-edged compliment if I ever got one." He looked at her as he hadn't done since that day in the hospital parking lot when he'd faced her for the first time as head of the Chemsly Citizens' Committee. Blue eyes narrowed into ominous slits glared down at her.

"Well, here's another. I'd like you to bring the coffee down here. First off, I don't want Jenny to be alone...and second I don't know if I can control myself alone in that big ol' house with a hunk like you."

She fluttered her eyelashes.

"Argh!" He rounded away from her and headed toward the house. Madison repressed a smirk. If he'd been a ten-year-old, he would have been stamping his feet.

Chapter Eleven

"So what did the autopsy on Jenny's cat reveal? Am I now a condemned pet murderer?" He handed her a cup of coffee and was glad he'd taken time to cool down before he returned. Her taunting remarks had roused such a crazy mix of emotions roiling around in his gut he couldn't decide if he wanted to kiss her or tell her to get the hell off his property. Man, no woman had ever upset him like this one.

"Actually…" She took a sip and stared down into the mug as he leaned against the fence with his. "It was antifreeze poisoning. Just before Jenny's dad ended up in the hospital, he put some in his truck. A bit leaked out onto the garage floor. Strange as it sounds, dogs and cats love the taste of the stuff. The little cat must have lapped it up. I told Jenny's mother, but we both thought it best not to tell her. We didn't want her blaming her father for what was an accident."

"Definitely. Let her blame me if she needs a scapegoat."

"I don't believe in casting blame where none is due."

Before he could respond, the child came out of the barn.

"Mr. Archer." She ran over to them. "It's a beautiful kitten. Thank you."

"Glad you like it. Now what about that ride?" He

handed Madison his cup. "Candy's ready and waiting."

"That would be great." She followed Clay into the paddock and let him boost her onto the mare.

"Want me to walk beside you?" he asked.

"No, I'll be fine. I'm cantering in my lessons now."

"Okay, only in western pleasure riding we call it loping." He grinned up at her and turned the sorrel mare loose.

Jenny urged Candy to a trot and headed around the ring. Clay watched her for a few moments, then called out, "Ask her to lope, if you feel comfortable."

The child did so and flashed him a broad grin as the mare responded.

"She's got a nice seat—" He started to comment on Jenny's riding ability but stopped short. Dr. Madison Todd had bent over and was tying her running shoe.

Ah, man, speaking of seats. And I was just getting cool after those suggestive remarks of hers. She's really out to give me one hell of a hard time.

Later, when Madison and Jenny had driven off down the lane, Clay Archer strode into his house and upstairs. In the bathroom he shucked his clothes and stepped into a cold shower.

****

"What are you doing here?" Madison's breath hiccupped out the words.

Standing on her mother's front porch in a brown suede jacket, green shirt, and tan Dockers was the last person she'd expected or wanted to see when she'd volunteered to answer the door.

"Your mother invited me to Thanksgiving dinner."

In one hand Clay Archer held an arrangement of autumn flowers, in the other a bottle of wine.

"Why?" The question was an exhale of exasperation.

"Madison, really!" Molly Todd appeared beside her daughter, taking Clay by the arm and drawing him into the warmth of the foyer. "It's Thanksgiving, and Mr. Archer was going to be all alone out at that big house. We couldn't allow that, now, could we?" She turned her most disarming smile on the man. "Come in, come in. You're just in time for one of Paige's famous martinis."

"Thanks." He stepped inside, and Madison closed the door a bit harder than necessary behind him. "These are for you." He held the flowers and wine out to Molly. "And it's Clay, not Mr. Archer."

"They're beautiful." Molly buried her nose in the blooms. "My favorite autumn colors. Thank you. Madison, take Clay's jacket, will you, while I find a vase for these lovely things."

She turned and headed toward the kitchen.

"Your jacket?" Madison held out her hand as her mother disappeared through the swinging door. She let the two words carry the exasperated sigh she'd suppressed in Molly's presence.

She shouldn't have been surprised to discover her mother had invited the enemy to dinner. It was typical of Molly Todd's generous nature. Now she'd have to respect her mother's decision by being polite and hospitable to the last person on earth with whom she wanted to spend Thanksgiving. Her mother would expect no less of her.

At least he's not wearing his cowboy outfit. No hat, no boots, no oh-so-fitted jeans.

"Thanks." He slipped out of the brown suede and

132

handed it to her.

Soft, expensive. She stifled a childish urge to fling it to the floor and stomp on it. She imagined she knew where the money had come from to buy it, and it turned her stomach.

"Come into the family room." She forced out the words after she'd hung the garment in the closet. "Jordan and the twins are there."

Could he sense the anger she was struggling to contain? She hoped he did.

"Twins?" Clay sounded surprised as he followed her toward the rear of the house.

"Jordan and my sister Paige have twins…Katie and Daniel," she replied, as the sound of children's laughter gushed out of the doorway.

She led him into the big sun-filled room decorated with comfortable-looking couches and easy chairs, an array of toys scattered over the carpet. Ceilidh, who'd been playing with the blond-haired boy and girl seated on the floor, stopped abruptly, looked up, and then raced over to Clay with an eager, welcoming bark.

"Hi, girl." Clay grinned and patted her head. "Good to see you, too."

"Welcome." Jordan Anderson got up from the leather recliner where he'd been watching football on a wide flatscreen television. Her brother-in-law showed no surprise at his boss's arrival.

"Thank you." Clay accepted Jordan's extended hand, and Madison assumed from her brother-in-law's composure that he'd known in advance about Molly's invitation to the mill owner. Probably Paige had been aware, as well. She most likely was the only one left uninformed.

The reason wasn't difficult to guess. Her mother had correctly assumed Madison wouldn't come if she'd known Clay Archer was to be their dinner guest, even though Thanksgiving was always a major family event.

"Martinis are ready." Paige entered from the kitchen carrying a tray with a pitcher and glasses.

"Mr. Archer, this is my wife, Paige." Jordan made the introduction. "And those two rowdies on the floor are our twins, Daniel and Katie."

"The name is Clay." He stepped forward to take the tray from Madison's sister and place it on the coffee table. "Nice to meet you, Paige. Hi, kids." He grinned at the small pair who'd stopped playing to stare up at him.

"You have horses," Daniel said. "Aunt Madison told us. Can we ride them sometime?"

"Daniel, it's not polite to ask for an invitation," Paige admonished gently.

"Sure you can," he replied. "Just as soon as your aunt says they're fit and I've gotten them used to being ridden again. Think you can wait that long?"

"I guess." Daniel looked doubtful.

"Martini, Clay?" Paige was pouring drinks into crystal glasses as Molly came into the room.

"Ah…" He hesitated.

"Beer?" Jordan grinned.

"Beer." Clay grinned back.

"Coming right up."

"Are you getting settled in, out at the estate?" As Jordan headed into the kitchen, Molly accepted the glass her daughter handed her, smiled at Clay, and indicated a chair opposite her.

"Pretty much."

He sat down, and Madison could see him relaxing, another victim of her family's affability. She'd seen it many times over the years. This was the first occasion she wished it didn't work so well.

"I'm sure you've been busy." Molly's gentle beauty was a soft glow Madison loved as she gazed at her mother. Even after the death of the man she'd loved for nearly forty years, Molly Todd still had the capacity to ignore her own pain and reach out to others. Everyone who knew Molly Todd loved and respected her. Madison was no exception.

In deference to those feelings, she'd be polite and hospitable to Clay Archer for this day. But for this day only. Tomorrow it would be back to business as usual, including her crusade against the mill.

****

A half hour later Molly stood and headed for the kitchen. "Excuse me, I have to check on dinner."

"I'll help." Paige got up to follow her mother.

"Me, too." Madison stood.

"Maybe you and Clay could take the twins for a walk in the park." Molly paused in the doorway. "Paige and I will manage. There really isn't room for three around the stove."

"Jordan and Clay can mind them." Madison felt a trap closing around her. "I'll set the table."

"Already done, and Jordan has promised to do a few minor repairs for me. So"—Molly raised her eyebrows and smiled—"it's up to you two."

"Please, Aunt Madison!" Daniel jumped to his feet and caught at her hand. "We can take Ceilidh. It'll be cool!"

"Well, all right. Get your coats and hats." She

glanced over at Clay. "You don't have to come."

"But I'd like to." He stood up and set his beer can aside. "I haven't had a chance to play in a park...ever."

****

Twenty minutes later, Madison sat on a park bench watching Clay build leaf castles for Daniel and Katie who, together with Ceilidh, floundered around in them, the two youngsters screaming in delight. For someone who had had no family life, Clay Archer certainly had a way with kids. He'd make a great father someday...with someone who wasn't Madison Todd.

The latter idea made something inside plummet. She had to struggle to force a smile when she saw Daniel and Katie racing toward her. Their faces were rosy from excitement and the crisp October day as they scrambled up beside her on the bench.

"Auntie Madison, can we go on the swings now?" Daniel asked. "Uncle Clay said he'd give us a push."

"Uncle Clay?" Madison looked up at Clay, who'd followed the pair, a broad grin on his face.

"Their chosen moniker." He shrugged. "I like it. Do you mind?"

"No, I guess not." She hitched one shoulder. "They have to call you something, and neither 'Clay' nor 'Mr. Archer' seems appropriate."

"Thanks. Makes me feel part of the family." He swung Katie up into his arms, and she giggled. "Now, let's go find those swings."

****

Later they headed back to Molly's house, Katie riding on Clay's shoulders, Daniel skipping along as he held Madison's hand and Ceilidh's leash.

Clay felt a happiness he'd never before

136

experienced enveloping him. He glanced over at Madison, her cheeks bright from the cold, and thought again how terrific she was. He wondered if passersby would mistake them for a family. He wouldn't mind if they did. He'd take pride in their misunderstanding. If someday he could have Madison and kids, he'd—

"Uncle Clay?" Interrupting his thoughts, Daniel peeked around Madison.

"What is it, buddy?" He adjusted Katie and grinned down at the eager little face.

"My dad told me you have your very own airplane. Can we have a ride in it some day?"

"It's not my airplane, but if your parents say it's okay, sure you can."

"And Aunt Madison, too?"

"Daniel…" Madison's tone was one of mild reproof.

"Sure, if she wants to come. I know I'd like it if she did." He grinned at her, all-out daring her.

"Come on, kids." She ignored him as they turned into her mother's drive. "I think I can smell turkey and pumpkin pie."

****

"Great dinner…as always, Molly." Jordan pushed back from the table and patted his middle. "Now I'll work some of it off cleaning up the rest of those leaves."

"I'll do the cleanup in here." Madison stood and began to gather up the dishes. "Mom, you and Paige can finish your coffee in the living room. You deserve a break."

"I'll help." Clay got to his feet and began to gather up plates.

"Thank you, Clay." Molly spoke as Madison opened her mouth to refuse his offer. "Madison ends up doing this chore alone every year. I'm sure she'll appreciate help. Won't you, darling?" She turned one of her most innocuous, dazzling smiles on her daughter. Madison gave up.

"Yes, okay, fine." She began clearing the table with a noisy vehemence that brought a sly smile to Paige's face as she and her mother headed into the living room.

"Come on, guys," Jordan called to the twins as he headed for the door. "You can help me with the leaves. Join us when you're finished in here, Clay."

"Will do."

Madison flinched. The man was fitting into her family like a hand into a perfectly cut glove. And they were all greasing his palm. Why couldn't they understand that their having a friendly relationship with Clayton Archer was outrageous?

He followed her into the kitchen and put his stack of plates and glasses on the counter above the dishwasher. As he started to return to the dining room, she stopped him.

"Don't get comfortable," she said blocking his way, hands on her hips.

"What?"

"I don't want you starting to feel you belong here, no matter how my family treats you."

"Okay." He crossed his arms on his chest and met her annoyed stare. "Sorry if I gave the wrong impression. This is the best Thanksgiving I've ever had. I didn't mean to get overly familiar. Maybe I should go help Jordan and the kids."

He swung past her, out toward the front of the house and the closet that held his jacket. Madison threw back her head and closed her eyes.

Don't let him soften you up.

She drew a deep breath and began to load the dishes into the washer. Think about *his* mill and all the damage it's doing. She paused and looked out the window to where Clay had joined Jordan, the twins, and Ceilidh, a rake in hand.

Think about Dad, she ordered herself as a last resort.

****

"Time to go, Daniel and Katie."

Paige leaned out the open kitchen window and called to the children busily piling up fallen leaves in the backyard with Clay and their father in the twilight.

"Coming, hon." Madison saw the smile Jordan's reply brought to her sister's lips as Paige ducked back inside and closed the window. Happiness, that's what they had, the kind that so far had eluded Dr. Madison Todd.

"Another great dinner, Mom." Paige pecked her mother on the cheek. "Thanks."

"I thank you for helping and Madison for doing the cleanup." Molly spread out her hands to indicate the spotless kitchen. "I knew there had to be some practical reason why I had two daughters."

The door opened, letting in a gush of crisp, cold autumn with Clay, Jordan, the twins, and the dog.

"I'll be heading out, too." Clay paused near the sink. "I have animals to see to, and I don't like to leave Chance alone too long. Thanks for a great dinner, Mrs. Todd."

"You're most welcome, Clay. Next time, bring Chance. This is a dog-friendly house."

Next time, next time! There won't be a next time, not if I have any share in making that decision. Madison stifled the words that raced across her mind at her mother's warm invitation.

"Will do." He turned and shook hands with Jordan. "Enjoyed the day, Jordan." He looked down at the twins, dusty and rosy-cheeked, and rumpled Daniel's hair. "Had a great time in the leaves, too, guys. Some day soon, my place and a horseback ride, okay?"

"Wow! Sure!" Daniel was ecstatic. "When?"

"As soon as I can get the horses in shape," he replied. "Your Aunt Madison will have to help me with that decision. Your whole family is invited." He shot a questioning glance at Madison. She deflected it by turning away.

"We'd love to come," Molly replied. "I haven't seen the Gregory place in years. It used to be such a lovely old house."

"And will be again, I hope. Paige"—Clay turned to Madison's sister—"Jordan told me you made the pumpkin pies. If you ever decide to start a business, Paige's Pumpkin Pies would be a sure thing."

"Is Archer an Irish name?" Paige laughed. "You have the gift, laddie." She rose on tiptoes and planted a light kiss on his cheek.

"I hardly think Paige is considering going into the bakery business." Madison could control herself no longer. "She's a chartered accountant, and a very good one. She's currently considering becoming the financial investigator for the Chemsly Citizens' Committee."

"Madison…" Her sister turned on her.

A stunned silence pervaded the room.

"Really?" Clay was the first to speak. "Keeping it all in the family, are you?"

There was no hint of rancor in his tone, only interest.

"I'm afraid Madison has jumped the gun, Clay." Paige gave her sister a what-do-you-think-you're-saying look. "I haven't decided to go back into practice. The twins still need me. Now, come on, Jordan, and bring those dusty little critters we call kids with you. They've had a full day. It's bath time."

****

Fifteen minutes later, when Madison finally found herself alone in the foyer with her mother, she turned to Molly, exasperation in her voice and expression.

"Why, Mom? Why on earth would you foist that man on us...on me...when you know..."

"Madison, darling, in spite of what you might think, Clayton Archer isn't a monster, only another human being...a lonely human being with no family and probably hardly any friends in Chemsly. When I found him buying a frozen turkey dinner in the supermarket, I couldn't do less than invite him to join us."

"Being you, no, definitely not...I suppose."

"Being a representative of Daniel Todd's family," she revised gently. "You know how your father expected us to treat those less fortunate."

"Less fortunate! Mom, the man owns a multi-million-dollar industry, lock, stock, and barrel! I'd hardly number him among the less fortunate!"

"I'm not talking about financially, and you know it, Madison." Molly gave her daughter a disparaging look.

"Okay, okay, I'm on your thought train…riding but not enjoying it." Madison reached into the closet and pulled out her jacket. "I've got to be going. Busy day at work tomorrow. Come on, Ceilidh."

"Good night, dear. Thanks for coming…and tolerating my indulgences." A whimsical little smile tipping her lips, she kissed her daughter on the cheek.

****

"Madison, wait!"

Clay Archer's voice stopped her as she fitted the key into the door of her Jeep. He stepped out of the shadows of the hedge at the end of her mother's drive and strode toward her in the encroaching darkness. "I have to talk to you."

"Let's leave it until our next official meeting." She managed to stifle the start his appearance had given her and opened the door of her vehicle. "I can't wait to see what nasty surprises you have in store."

"This can't wait." His hand shot out and shoved it shut. Ceilidh, by her mistress's side, growled.

"Sorry, girl." He looked down at the dog.

"What do you think you're doing?" Madison snapped, swinging to face him. "I had to be civil to you in there, but out here…"

She couldn't finish. He'd pulled her into his arms and was kissing her so passionately she lost her balance and would have fallen if he hadn't been holding her in a powerful grip.

Electrical currents flared as Dr. Madison Todd once again became mesmerized by her sworn enemy.

"Oh, God, Madison!" he breathed against her hair when he finally allowed her to come up for air.

"Clay…" She struggled to come to her senses, his

name a choked word. "This is crazy. It won't work, and we both know it."

"Speak for yourself, Doctor." His lips against her temple spoke in a tone so soft, so utterly suggestive Madison's senses whirled. "I'm willing to give it one hell of a try."

"Don't be foolish! It's just a crazy hot attraction that flares up like fireworks between us. It'll fizzle just as quickly if we pursue it. It's got absolutely no future."

She backed out of his arms, stepped away from him, and ran a hand through her hair. "Why did you come here anyway? How could you show your face in my mother's house after what you did to my family at that meeting?"

He stuffed his hands into his pockets and shrugged. "I didn't have any other invitations, your family is extremely broadminded, and in spite of what you're trying to do to my mill, I wanted to see you again outside of a working situation. Guess I like fireworks."

In the shadowed twilight she saw him grin.

"Okay, you've had your family dinner and your fireworks…as much of them as you'll ever get." She had to talk harsh and hard. Even without his cowboy getup, the man was far too attractive, far too appealing in the soft autumn evening, a full moon rising over his shoulder.

"Okay." He pulled his truck keys from his pocket. "But on that last bit, I know you're dead wrong."

He turned and strode off toward his truck parked at the curb, whistling "You Light Up My Life."

****

All right, Joe Cool. So you pulled off the casual act. Clever, aren't you! What now?

143

Clay wasn't whistling as he drove toward the estate in the darkness, his thoughts making him grimace. That kiss, like the previous two, had been a stupid move. For sure it had done little to enhance Madison's opinion of him.

She'd brought it on herself, he argued. She'd been so damned appealing all afternoon, playing with the twins and Ceilidh at the park, her face bright and glowing in the crisp afternoon air. And later, joking and teasing with Paige and Jordan at dinner, her obvious loving concern for her mother making her be hospitable to him on her account… The list went on and on.

As he drove out of range of the town's streetlights, clouds drifted in to cover the moon, and his headlights pierced an inky blackness. It had been a beautiful autumn day, but now a sharp, cold chill filled the air. Prime conditions for a lightning storm, he thought, and drove a little faster. He wanted to get the animals tended before it hit. He shouldn't have left Chance alone, but the dog was still recovering, and he felt too many new people and too much excitement might be bad for him.

Maybe if he kept himself really busy, he'd manage to work Dr. Madison Todd out of his mind…at least for a little while.

****

"Madison, can you come over right away? I need you to look after the twins."

The urgent tone of her mother's voice startled Madison to full wakefulness as she struggled up on one elbow, clutching the phone.

"Mom? Why? What's happened? Where's Paige… and Jordan?" A cold wave of fear washed over her.

144

"Jordan woke up a short time ago not feeling well. He got up to go to the bathroom and collapsed. They've taken him by ambulance to the hospital. Paige is with him, but Steve...Dr. McLean...called to say he could use my help. So if you could come over to Paige's house and stay with the twins..."

"Yes, of course." Madison was already out of bed and struggling into her slippers. "I'll be there in fifteen minutes."

She punched End and dropped the cordless phone onto the dresser as she bolted toward her clothes hanging over the back of a chair. As she pulled on her jeans, she could feel her blood pressure rising.

"This is it!" she muttered to Ceilidh, who'd awakened in her place on the end of her bed. "I won't let Clay Archer and his mill murder another person I love! From now on my battle to close that mass killer is going to get highly visible...and physical!"

****

"When is Daddy coming home, Auntie Madison?" Katie looked up at her with wide, questioning eyes as Madison zipped up her pink quilted jacket. "I miss him and Mommy."

"Soon, I hope, sweetie." Madison pecked a kiss on the pert little nose and tried to avoid the lost, puzzled expression on the little girl's face.

"Peanut butter and jelly." Daniel peered into his brown lunch sack. "Wow! Thanks, Aunt Madison. It's my favorite."

"You're welcome." Madison straightened up, grinned, and patted him on the head. "You're my favorite nephew, right? You deserve the best. Come on, now, into the car. I have to get you both to school."

"Can Ceilidh ride in the back with us?" Katie was fastening the leash on the little dog.

"Sure, why not? It'll be a treat for her."

"Come on, Ceil." The little girl headed out the back door, pink Cinderella pack sack on her back, the dog on its lead trotting beside her.

"Aunt Madison?" Daniel held her back as she reached for her keys.

"Yes, Daniel?"

"I'm really worried…about Dad. I woke up when they took him away. There were lights flashing, and sirens, and Mommy was all white and shaking." He looked up at her, blue eyes round with concern. "He is going to be okay, isn't he, Aunt Madison?"

"Grammy and Dr. McLean are taking care of him," she replied, hunkering down in front of him, her hands on his small shoulders. "And we both know how good they are."

He paused and stared at her for a moment before melting into her arms.

"I'm scared, Aunt Madison," he said, his words muffled against her shoulder. "I just don't want Katie to know. I love my Dad…a lot."

"We all do." Madison held him tight and had a difficult time replying over the lump in her throat. "He knows it, and that will help him get well."

"I'll make him a big happy face card in school today." He pulled back from her, his face brightening through his tears. "I'll print 'We love you' in big, big letters. That'll help, won't it?"

"Definitely." Madison pulled a Kleenex from her pocket and wiped his eyes before holding it to his nose. "Blow. We can't let Katie see us upset, can we?"

****

After she'd left the twins in the care of their classroom teacher, she sat in her little SUV in the school parking lot and punched Tom's number into her cell. A plan for the rest of her day in mind, she needed his help.

"Tommy, there's been an emergency," she told him the moment he answered. "Jordan's collapsed. He's in intensive care at the hospital. Mom and Paige are with him. I've dropped the twins off at school, but I won't be able to pick them up at two thirty. Can you? And keep them until suppertime, maybe later? Thanks. You're terrific."

Satisfied the children would be well taken care of, she punched End and hurried on with her next call to put her plan into action.

Chapter Twelve

Clay Archer inched his truck through the crowd of onlookers and eased to a stop beside a trio of RCMP cruisers. Ahead of him, blocking the mill gate, was a group of placard-wielding protesters. Panning their lenses over them were two television camera crews and a half dozen other media types. Leading the slogan-chanting pickets was—who else?—Dr. Madison Todd.

Incredible. He shook his head. *The woman is absolutely incredible.* He shut off the engine and pulled the key from the ignition. With a heaved sigh, he swung out of his vehicle. *This is going to be a mess.*

"Clay, boy, sorry to drag you away from those renovations out at the estate." Rick Reid strode toward him. A gleaming BMW, a long scratch down its side, was parked a few feet away. "But I thought you should see with your own eyes before I have the police clear it away."

"How long has this been going on?" Clay removed his sunglasses and squinted into the eleven a.m. sunlight.

"A couple of hours now. They were here when I arrived around nine o'clock and refused to let me in." He looked over at Clay and suddenly chuckled. "Damned if I don't get a kick out of sparring with Maddy. She's one hell of an opponent. Just wish she hadn't scratched my car."

"I don't see much humor in the situation...especially with the media out in force." Clay rested his hands on his hips and surveyed the situation.

"Media be damned! One day in the press and it'll all be forgotten. The trick is not to let Maddy come off lookin' like a blessed martyr." Rick Reid's mouth quirked up at one corner. "That's why I told the police to hold off on forcin' a confrontation until there's absolutely no other way. I think we can wait 'em out, just don't let any food or drink through. And no access to washrooms."

"I don't know..." Clay didn't like the sound of the tactics, but just then Madison broke ranks. Leaving her companions to carry on marching and chanting, she headed for Clay and the mill manager, a large placard supported by a 2x2 resting on her shoulder.

"Mr. Archer, how nice of you to finally show up," she yelled, drawing the media into a curious circle around them. "I trust you're here to present us with a plan that will put an end to the noxious emissions belching out of this death trap you call a mill!"

"I'm here to talk." Clay wasn't about to back down publicly. "Bring your people inside. We'll get you hot coffee and a comfortable place to settle this disagreement."

"Behind closed doors?" She guffawed. "I think not. I want the media to hear just exactly what it is you're prepared to do. Or not do."

"Sorry." He crossed his arms on his chest and faced her squarely. "That's my only offer."

"Well, then, fine! Here's my answer..."

Before anyone could stop her, Madison strode over to where Clay had left the company truck. Using her placard as a weapon, she swung it with all her strength against the shining grill. Headlights shattered. She swung again and a fender bent.

"Hold it! Hold it just a damn minute!" He grabbed her and wrested the sign out of her hands as cameras rolled and flashed.

"Oh, so it's not so nice when something of *yours* gets damaged, is it?" She was struggling in his grasp, her face livid with fury. "And that's only a truck! What if it was your father…or your brother-in-law?"

"Brother-in-law?" Clay didn't understand.

"Don't pretend you don't know Jordan is in intensive care!"

"Sweet Jesus, Jordon's in the hospital? When? What…?"

"Miss, we're going to have to place you under arrest." An officer moved between the two and clamped his hand on her shoulder. "Willful destruction of property."

"That won't be necessary, Officer." Clay took a step back and tried to appear cool and controlled. "The vehicle belongs to my company. I won't be preferring charges."

"But I am." Rick Reid joined the group. "She keyed my car when I tried to get into the mill earlier. It'll cost a bloody fortune to get it fixed."

"You saw her?" Clay swung on him. News of Jordan's hospitalization had set his nerves jangling.

"She was in the front lines when I was tryin' to get through."

"Come along, miss." Another officer supported his colleague. "We'll let a judge sort this out."

Again, cameras flashed and rolled. Exasperated,

Clay pulled his Stetson lower over his eyes. There was nothing more he could do. He had to stand and watch as Madison was handcuffed and herded into a squad car with full media coverage.

****

"Madison, what have you done now!" Exasperation exploded from Paige Anderson's words as the constable escorted her into the cellblock. She carried a newspaper.

"Paige! At last! Now I can finally get out of here." Madison clutched the bars of the second of the two small cages. "I thought you'd never get here. How's Jordan?"

"As well as can be expected." She crossed her arms on her chest and stared at her younger sister. "Madison, what in the world has gotten into you? Vandalism, for heaven's sake! And to not one but *two* Glendon Forest Products vehicles. What are you, thirteen?"

"That mill is killing your husband like it killed our father." Madison's knuckles whitened as her hands clutched the bars of her cell. "I won't let that happen, even if it means doing crazy things that will get into the media and attract public sympathy to our cause."

"Oh, Madison." Paige shook her head. "Jordan collapsed from exhaustion and a congenital heart problem. His illness has nothing to do with the mill."

"It doesn't?" Madison's grip on the bars relaxed. "But I thought…"

"Yes, and you acted on that thought way too reflexively. Now look at you."

"So I made a slight mistake." Madison's fighting spirit rose again. "It was for the best. Got a lot of publicity, didn't it?"

"It certainly did. Not only were you on the provincial television news last evening, look at this."

She snapped open the folded newspaper and held the front page in front of her sister. A photo of her raging at Clay dominated.

" 'Crusader versus Cowboy,' " she read aloud. " 'Alberta ranch foreman and CEO of Glendon Forest Products Clay Archer spars with Chemsly veterinarian Dr. Madison Todd during a recent dustup between mill executives and local citizens' committee.' I look really incensed, don't I?"

"Yes, and how do you think Mom is enjoying it?"

"Oh."

"Yes. Oh. Madison, I think it's high time you started to face the reality of what your campaign is doing to her. She's been through enough."

"But…"

"No buts. Just stop it. Now is there anything you need? I'll drop it off later."

"Need? Paige, what are you talking about? Get me out of here!"

"Sorry. There's nothing I can do until Judge Arseneau gets back to town tomorrow morning. You have to be arraigned."

"You're enjoying this, aren't you." Madison glared out at her sister.

"No, but if it will stop your tilting at windmills…"

"Well, it won't. Nothing short of closing down Clay Archer's mill will satisfy me."

"Okay, fine. See you in the morning. Officer, I'm ready to leave." Paige's voice rose to hail the officer on duty. She thrust the paper through the bars to her sister. "Keep it and give it some very serious thought."

Chagrined, Madison could only watch as her sister walked away, the heavy door of the cellblock clanging shut behind her.

****

The minute Clay Archer stepped into the cell area and saw her sitting hunched up alone on a bench in a corner, his stomach lurched. This wasn't what he wanted, not at all.

"Hello," he said.

"Come to gloat, have you?" She sprang to her feet, eyes flashing her feelings as she faced him through the bars.

"No."

"You have ten minutes," the officer who'd escorted him into the cellblock informed him and left.

"Then why? Do you have some kinky fetish about seeing women held prisoner?"

"You really know how to hit below the belt, don't you?" He removed his Stetson and stood holding it in both hands. "I came to tell you I'm sorry about Jordan...and to see if I could get you released on the grounds of your providing an essential community service...you are the only vet in Chemsly."

"I take it your idea didn't fly with the authorities?"

"No." He shook his head and looked down at his boots. "They said they'd put a notice on the local radio station saying you're unavailable until further notice. It provided the phone number of a vet about twenty miles from here to call in case of an emergency. Furthermore, until this town's one and only judge gets back from his fishing trip tomorrow there's nothing I can do."

"Argh!" Madison's frustration grated out through clenched teeth as she jerked her hands into fists at her

153

sides.

"Well, what did you expect?" Exasperation made him snap back. "You tried to trash my truck."

"Only as a last resort, and only because…" Her voice trailed off.

"Yeah, I know. You thought your family was losing someone else because of the mill."

"That doesn't change the fact that those poisonous emissions *did* kill my father and God only knows how many others. So why don't you just get the hell out of here?"

"Fine." *Bloody hell, there's no reasoning with the woman*. "Officer," he called. "I'm ready to leave."

He slapped his hat back on his head and left without giving her a backward glance.

****

Madison jumped to her feet as the door of the cell block clanged open. She was more than ready to go home. The night had been anything but restful. A drunk deposited in the cell opposite her had spent the entire time vomiting and raging. He'd passed out an hour ago, but the stench emanating from his area was too appalling to allow her to rest.

Surprise overwhelmed her eagerness when Clay Archer entered with Paige and an officer.

"What are you doing here…again?" She stared at him.

"I thought your sister might appreciate my assistance in getting the charges against you dismissed."

"Paige is a smart lady." She faced him defiantly as the officer worked the lock on her cell. "I'm sure she didn't need…"

"And I'm sure I did." Paige, dressed in a navy suit that was both professional and becoming to her slender figure, contradicted. "Clay was a big help in expediting the process. I haven't got all morning to spend bailing you out of this mess, Madison. I have a job interview at ten thirty with Milton and Washington, Chartered Accountants."

"Paige, you're going back to work?" Madison stepped out of the cell, as the door swung open, and seized her sister by the shoulders. "That's great!"

"Only part time," she replied. "The twins are in school most of the day now, and…" She hesitated. "I want to reduce the financial burden on Jordan."

"I think you're making an excellent decision." Madison drew her into a hug. "And once you're settled in…"

"One day at a time." Paige held her sister out at arm's length. "Let's just get you out of here and me to that interview."

****

"Wish me luck." Paige waved to Clay and Madison as they parted company outside the courthouse.

"Of course!" Madison paused to watch her sister climb into her minivan and drive away.

"Your sister was impressive in there just now." Clay gestured back at the courthouse. "That was quite a feat, getting this incident expunged."

"Wait until you see her in action going over Glendon Forest Products' accounts."

"A dubious expectation, at best. I doubt any court in this country will give her the right to examine my company's financial statements, but I'll let you have your fantasy. Even the RCMP would have trouble getting such access, since there's no evidence of wrongdoing."

He had to hang tough. He'd felt himself turning to jelly when he'd seen her in that cell the previous day, her clothes disheveled, her hair in a tangled mass of curls. She'd looked so innocent and pretty and, yeah, downright sexy. He couldn't risk any further softening of his resolves, or the next thing he knew he'd be giving her the password to the company computer.

"Fantasies can come true if a person believes in them and works hard enough to make them realities. Now I've got to call a cab. I need to get home, shower, and return to work."

She started to turn away, but he stopped her.

"I'll drive you," he said his hand on her arm. "I have a truck."

"Not *the* truck? I can't be seen riding around in that tribute to Glendon Forest Products."

"No, it's a loaner, with no logos. The one you tried to destroy is in the shop. You did a great job on its headlights and fender. Come on, let's go."

****

"Step on it," she ordered as he pulled away from the curb.

"Still afraid someone will see us together?"

"Definitely." She avoided the amused grin he shot in her direction and stared straight ahead.

"You can always cower under the dash," he suggested, stopping at a red light.

"Cower! Hardly. I just don't have time to answer a whole lot of questions about why I'm driving around with you on the morning after I trashed your truck."

"Ah, ha! So you admit it! Wish I had that on tape."

156

"The light's green. Go, go, go. I feel as if I've been wearing these clothes for a month."

****

"Madison, wait." He stopped the truck in the dooryard of her bungalow. The way she grabbed the door handle indicated her eagerness to escape.

"What?" The word was a weary, impatient monosyllable.

"We've got to stop the dramatics and get down to some serious negotiating. When can we meet, just you and me, to talk?"

"So you're ready to negotiate?" She swung to face him. "Seems my so-called dramatics have been successful. What happened? Did Glendon Forest Products get a bad rap in the media as a result of what happened yesterday?"

"A little. But that's not important. Madison, you and I have this wild chemistry going on between us." He released his seatbelt and turned to face her, one arm resting on the top of the steering wheel. "I'd like to go with it, see where it takes us. But I can't, we can't, with this mill problem between us."

"Wild chemistry? Ha! Where did you get that idea? A few kisses—inspired, no doubt, by your macho self-image. Come on."

"So that's what you think it was?" *Another kick in the gut.*

"Look, I've had experience with a man like you, and I don't plan to repeat it. Sure, kissing you was fun and, to be honest, you're pretty darned good at it. But that's the end of it. Next time you try something like that, you'll know the meaning of having a face soundly slapped."

157

"Okay, okay, this macho bum will leave you alone."

"Fine." She opened the door into a day that had begun with bright sunshine but was fast becoming grey and overcast, full of threatening charcoal clouds. "Now, if you'll excuse me, I have plans to make."

"What kind of plans?"

"You'll have to wait and see." Favoring him with a sly smile, she slammed the truck door.

"Great." The word reeked of exasperation.

He watched until she'd disappeared into the house, then shifted into reverse and rammed his foot onto the gas pedal to send the truck shooting out of the yard. Frustration chafed him like starched underwear as he swung onto the road and gunned the engine. Tires squealed.

Real mature. Acting like a kid on his first hot date, and now tire spinning. Hell and damnation. That woman will be the ruination of me. And what did she mean, she had experience with a man like me?

In the distance, a bolt of lightning cracked the clouds, and he heard a distant rumble of thunder. Great! Another dry-as-a-bone storm.

****

Clay unlocked the door of his house and for a moment failed to respond to Chance's greeting. His thoughts were back with Madison and what her next move would be. Hell, it could be anything. With a resigned sigh, he turned his attention to the bouncing dog.

"Sorry, buddy. Didn't mean to ignore you, but that woman is driving me nuts. I've got to go ahead with my plans for the rehab centre, but she's not going to make it easy."

He went into the kitchen and opened a packet of gourmet dog food for Chance. Then he poured a bowl of ice water and set both on the floor.

"When we were living out on the range, bet you never dreamed there was stuff like that." He grinned as he watched his friend wolfing down what looked and smelled like a rich beef stew. "Well, you've stuck with me though the tough spots. Now you deserve the best."

He opened the stainless steel refrigerator, took out a beer, and paused to glance at the other gleaming new appliances scattered around the otherwise dilapidated kitchen. He needed an interior decorator, and bad. Someone who could make a blend of the old and new and sort out this weird mix he had going. He knew the perfect person. All he had to do was convince her his mill was perfectly safe and that he was the man of her dreams.

His mouth quirked into a sardonic grin. St. George had had it easy. All he'd had to do was kill a dragon or two. First he'd polish off this beer. Afterwards he'd head down to the barn to tend the horses and cats.

****

He pulled off his boots inside the door and headed for the refrigerator. Barn work done, Chance fed, Madison out of jail. He was ready to relax and watch a bit of television and forget the woman. Snapping the tab on a beer, he wandered into the parlor, where a wide-screen TV sat in a corner. With a groan, he sank into the ancient wing chair opposite it, picked up the remote, and turned on a local news broadcast.

"This evening we'll be interviewing Dr. Madison Todd."

Clay choked on his beer as the anchorman continued, "Dr. Todd, a respected veterinarian, is well known for her battle to stop Glendon Forest Products from *allegedly* further polluting our environment. She's graciously agreed to be interviewed this evening to defray some of the negative publicity that has recently surrounded her efforts. Good evening, Dr. Todd."

"Good evening, Peter." The camera switched to Madison. Clay groaned.

Wearing a pale pink dress trimmed with demure white lace, her hair tied back with a matching ribbon that allowed a few curls to frame her delicately featured face, Dr. Madison Todd looked like an angel, a breathtaking angel. And everyone knows angels don't lie.

"Ah, man!" Clay shifted in his chair and had a half-decent idea of what he was in for. No one made an angel look bad in print. No one sent an angel to jail. Not unless he was the devil incarnate.

He'd never seen her dressed like that. She'd probably rushed out to buy that outfit especially for this occasion the minute after he'd driven away. She'd most likely plotted this entire scenario while she was in jail.

"Dr. Todd, you've recently cut a rather, shall we say, bellicose image in the media. You've been photographed casting malevolent glances at Clayton Archer, the new owner and CEO of Glendon Forest Products, in a meeting between mill representatives and your committee. And more recently, TV cameras filmed you doing battle with a company truck." The anchorman's expression suggested he found wry humor in the latter. "Would you care to explain?"

"Certainly, Peter. I thank you for giving me the

opportunity." Madison looked directly into the camera, the soul of sincerity. "I'm afraid my enthusiasm to rid Chemsly of a major and highly toxic source of pollution overwhelmed me. I apologize. Acting badly, even if it is in a good cause, isn't acceptable." She gave a wan little smile.

"Bring on the Oscar." Clay muttered and took a major gulp of beer.

"Perhaps it's Clayton Archer, Glendon Forest Products' new owner, and Rick Reid, the mill manager, who should be apologizing to you, Doctor. Weren't you recently incarcerated on charges laid by them?" The anchor's question displayed flagrant bias...at least in Clay's opinion. But then the guy was looking into that cherubic face.

"They were only doing what they saw as necessary to stall my campaign." She spoke softly and again turned into the camera as it zoomed in on her. "And while I don't agree with it, I understand their position."

"Ready for my close-up, Mr. DeMille." Clay ground out the classic line.

"But..." She turned back to the interviewer, her tone brightening. "That doesn't for a moment mean my committee and I will be relenting in our campaign. In fact, we'll be upping our efforts within the next few days."

"Would you care to share those plans with our viewers, Doctor?"

"Not at this time. I believe in the element of surprise."

"Sounds as if you've got a major event waiting in the wings. We'll be watching with interest." The interviewer turned back to the camera. "Our thanks to

Dr. Madison Todd for coming in this evening and clarifying Glendon Forest Products' seemingly over-zealous reaction to a legal demonstration. We wish Dr. Todd and her committee every success in their anti-pollution crusade."

The segment ended with a still photo of Madison sitting in her jail cell.

"Argh!" Clay snapped off the set and chugged the rest of his beer.

What kind of one-sided yellow journalism had that been? Peter Whoever-he-was had been thoroughly finessed by one totally charming, wholesomely gorgeous woman who knew how to wear a pink dress and when to look the soul of sincerity.

****

"Are you out to ruin me in front of this community?"

Madison flinched as his voice boomed out of her phone. She'd been curled up in her favorite PJs and had just finished watching the interview taped earlier in the day. She'd expected a reaction from him, in fact, hoped for one, just not as fast and hard as this. Her heartbeat headed into a lope, adrenaline rushing ready for battle.

"You and Rick Reid tried to use the media against our campaign." She hoped her tone was cool and even, not vibrating with the challenge surging through her body. "Are you saying I can't use it as well?"

"You know damn well what I mean. That get-up, the butterfly eyelashes, and the final zinger, that picture of you in jail. Get real, Doctor!"

"My dress, my eyelashes, my picture. All the real deal. Sorry if you can't handle it."

The line fell silent. Then, finally, "Look here,

Madison, this public sparring isn't getting us anywhere. You and I have to talk this out, go on a tour of the mill…"

"I've seen your mill, thank you very much, and I wasn't impressed. Now, if you were willing to open your books to my sister's scrutiny, prove to her beyond a shadow of a doubt that Rick didn't buy off any politicians…"

"Definitely not. I trust Rick."

"Well, bloody medals all over you for being the most gullible man on the planet. Wait until you see my next move."

"What adolescent trick have you got up your sleeve now? You've already trashed my truck. Would I be correct in assuming you plan to toilet-paper my house?"

Good. She had Clay Archer worried.

"Let me surprise you."

"Ahhh!"

"Good night, Mr. Archer. Pleasant dreams."

She clicked her cell shut, smirking. *Bet I'd make a great card player.* Her smile faded. *Wish I knew what I was going to do next.*

Lightning flashed through the room. Thunder rattled the windows.

"Let's pray for rain, Ceilidh," she said as she headed off to bed, the dog at her heels. "With the woods this dry, there'd be no stopping a forest fire."

****

Hours later, Clay awoke to the harsh ringing of his bedside phone. It was pitch dark. *What time is it?* He fumbled for the receiver.

"Yeah?" He propped himself up on an elbow as he spoke.

"Clay, boy, sorry to wake you at this ungodly hour, but we've got us an all-out emergency." It was Rick Reid's voice. "Damn storm. Near as we can tell, a lightnin' strike started a fire back in the bush about thirty miles north of town. Right now there's one hell of a blaze underway. You know anything about flyin' a water bomber, buddy? We sure could use another pilot."

****

"Madison?"

He rummaged in a drawer for a clean shirt, the phone crunched between his shoulder and his ear, as he heard her sleep-husky voice on the line.

"Clay? What time is it?" Then, more sharply, "What's wrong?"

"There's a forest fire back in the bush." He dragged out a grey sweatshirt and gave it a shake. "I'm going to fly a water bomber. Will you take care of Chance while I'm gone?"

"Sure, of course." She didn't hesitate. "Bring him to the airport with you. I'll meet you there in a half hour." A hesitation, then, "Clay?"

"Yeah?"

"Flying one of those old planes can be tricky. I hope you know what you're doing. Take care." The words were sincere and unvarnished. They caught him in the gut.

"You got it. See you shortly."

Damn, damn, damn. He wrenched the shirt over his head and reached for his boots. She cared, he cared. But she hadn't tried to stop him. She understood he had to go. Quite a woman, Madison Todd. If it weren't for that cursed mill and his need for its profits...

He picked up the phone again, hit number eight on the speed dial, and waited for Tom Mills to answer. Much as he wished he didn't have to, he knew he had to ask the farrier to look after the horses and cats while he was away. He couldn't expect Madison with the obligations of her practice to do it, but Chance still wasn't completely healed. The dog might need her expertise.

Chapter Thirteen

With the first streaks of dawn lightening the sky, he found her waiting in the airport parking lot beside her Jeep. The air was full of the acrid smell of burning. An ominous smoke haze covered the sky. When he stopped his pickup, she strode over to join him. She wore a grey jogging suit and sneakers, her hair scrunched back into an untidy ponytail.

"Sorry about this," he said when she bent to snap a leash on Chance's collar. "But I couldn't leave him alone, not in the shape he's in."

"Of course you couldn't." She straightened up, and the understanding in her eyes blew him away.

If I come back alive, I swear I'll find some way to make this thing between us work.

"Look, I know we didn't part on the best of terms last night, and I know we've got some pretty big issues between us…" He fumbled to a stop, not sure where he was going. He wasn't about to recant his decisions or apologize for them.

"There's a more immediate concern to address right now." She knelt to scratch Chance behind his ears, and the dog flogged his tail in appreciation. "So go. Chance and I will wait and see you off."

"Okay. Thanks." He put all the sincerity he was feeling into the second word. "Be good for Dr. Todd, fella," he said, looking down at the collie. "I'll be back to get you before you have time to miss me, promise." He turned and walked into the building without looking back.

Inside was a flurry of activity as pilots and ground crew sought to coordinate efforts. They clustered around a big, barrel-chested man in a plaid shirt and bush pants who stood holding a clipboard in the center of the room. Yelling out instructions, he waved his arms in various directions and sent men hurrying off.

"You the man in charge?" Clay asked.

"Yeah, who are you?"

"Clay Archer. Rick Reid asked me to fly one of the water bombers. I've got a pilot's license and some experience in the bush."

"Oh, yeah, right. Rick mentioned you'd be coming. There's a TBM Avenger on the far left outside the door, loaded and ready for takeoff. That's your baby."

"TBM Avenger? World War Two veteran?"

"Exactly. Bit temperamental, but overall a good craft. We have to use every bit of equipment we can muster. But if you don't think you can handle it…" He ran his gaze up and down Clay's sweatshirt, jeans, and cowboy boots.

"No problem. Speaking of Rick, I expected to see him here." He glanced around at the men in the waiting room.

"He was here. Took off first thing in a Cessna, with one of our best pilots, to evaluate the burn and come up with a plan to fight it."

"A Cessna? Pretty small plane to handle the up and down drafts that occur over a blaze."

"Yeah, well, Rick never was afraid of much. Now, that Avenger's waiting, and the sooner we start

167

dumping retardant on that fire the better, so…"

"Sure, sure, I'm going." He headed toward the door leading to the runways.

"Oh, and Archer?" The operations organizer stopped him.

"Yeah?"

"Good luck…and thanks."

****

Clay adjusted his headset, settled in his seat, and looked over the instrument panel in front of him. A bit of a challenge, but he'd manage…he hoped. Glancing out the window, he saw Madison standing near the terminal building, Chance sitting alert at the end of his leash by her side. She'd managed to force her way through the confusion to find a place to see him off.

He grinned and raised a hand to the pair. She replied with a half-wave, half-salute that made his heart lurch.

As if I'm going off to war. Well, I am headed off to battle a blaze…

He brought himself back to the moment as a voice in his headphones told him he was cleared for takeoff. Tucking thoughts of Madison Todd and Chance away, he settled back in the seat and began checking gauges, adjusting instruments, and mentally reviewing all he knew about flying this kind of mission. He'd flown water bombers in Alberta, but never one of this vintage.

He was well aware of the dangers. Flames could reach as high as two hundred feet into the smoke-choked air, and convection currents from the fire could cause unbelievable turbulence. As the heated air roared skyward, cooler air was sucked in at the base of the fire, causing high, erratic winds that could send a plane spinning earthward in seconds.

Increasing the danger were snags. These tall, dead trees often stuck out high above the forest canopy and tended to be invisible in dense smoke, only to suddenly appear directly in a bomber's path. Since a typical bombing run took place at a mere one hundred feet above tree level, these could prove disastrous.

During the final part of the run, he'd have approximately five seconds to swoop down, drop his load of retardant, and get out, yet he had to be on the lookout for ground crews. A payload of retardant weighed about twenty-four and a half tons and could reach a speed of one hundred meters per hour before it hit the ground. If he saw people below, he'd have to abort his mission.

Flying a bombing run could be like riding a bucking horse through a firestorm.

****

Madison pulled off her smock and rolled her shoulders in an effort to ease the tension haunting them. With the town engulfed in a thick smoke haze and the acrid smell of burning forest, nerves were on edge—and justifiably so, she thought as she hung her lab coat on its hanger.

The fire burned a mere twenty miles from town now, heading away from it in a southwesterly direction, but it would only take a change in the wind to put Chemsly in its path. Already, on the advice of the Emergency Measures Organization, a number of people had packed up and left. There'd been no official evacuation order, but that could come at any moment.

She looked down at Chance, lying alert and ready by her desk. The dog had been tense all day. Even

Ceilidh's attempts to distract him had failed.

He knows Clay's in danger.

A thrill of fear shuddered though her. With an effort, she brought herself up short. Clay Archer wasn't anything to her and never would be. He was the enemy, for God's sake. She gave herself a brisk mental shake.

****

When she stepped out into the street from her office, Chance's leash around her wrist, Ceilidh at her heels, sharp traces of burning rushed into her lungs and made her cough. She locked her surgery and hurried toward her SUV.

From somewhere overhead, deep in the thick charcoal fog, came the drone of a water bomber. Madison paused a moment at the door of her vehicle, listened…and wondered if it was Clay's plane. Those ancient aircraft were barely flight worthy, and flying one over a raging forest fire…

Enemy be damned. She cared.

With Chance in the rear seat and Ceilidh riding in her usual place as shotgun, Madison headed for her house on the edge of town. Forced to drive slowly through smoke at times blanket-thick, she became ensnarled in a traffic of heavily loaded vehicles, entire families with their most valued possessions crowded inside, headed away from the town.

She wished her mother had gone with Paige and the children when they left Chemsly earlier in the afternoon. But nothing, she knew, would have persuaded a nurse of Molly Todd's dedication to leave Dr. McLean's side under the circumstances. She knew her place in a time of emergency.

****

Madison turned into her driveway, parked, and hustled the dogs inside. Passing a radio, she snapped it on. She'd feed and water the dogs while she listened to the latest news report. If she had to hit the road to escape the fire, she wanted the animals nourished for the trip.

"...spreading rapidly, high wind currents directly over the fire making work difficult for retardant bombers," a newscaster's voice informed her.

Madison's stomach gave a sickly lurch as she placed a bowl of water on the floor for the dogs. Clay was up there somewhere in those treacherous wind currents, above a raging inferno, where one wrong move could...

An impatient knocking at her back door snapped her out of her thoughts.

"Hey, Maddy, it's me."

"Come on in, Tommy. It's not locked. And I'm decent." She tried to lighten her tone as she shushed the dogs' barking.

Smudged with soot from head to toe, he stepped inside and shut the door against the filthy air.

"Tommy, you're with a ground crew?" She recognized the attire. "What about your horses, the estate's horses, the cat and her kittens?"

"Not to worry, I've got it covered," he replied, remaining on the mat inside the door. "I moved all of Archer's animals to my place—it's a lot farther from the fire than the estate—and Jake Morgan is standing by with his tractor trailer in case they have to be evacuated. Anyway, that's not what I came to tell you. Maddy, there's been an accident. Clay Archer's plane went down about an hour ago...somewhere near the head of the fire."

****

Nerves on edge, Madison loaded the dogs into her vehicle. Something that felt like a jagged rock hurt in her chest. *Clay crashed at the head of the fire*. The thought kept hammering around in her head, producing nightmare images of possibilities.

Dear God, let him be okay, just let him be okay.

After piling in a couple of suitcases, she added medical supplies, as well as food and water for both herself and the animals. If an evacuation order came through while she was at the airport, she'd be ready.

"It's crazy for you to go out there, Maddy," Tom had argued. "You can't help. For cryin' out loud, you don't even like the guy." There was a pause. "Do you?"

"Look, I'm concerned about my dealings with the mill executive." She'd continued to rummage through her cupboard for nonperishable food. "I'm getting familiar with how Clay Archer operates. I don't want to have to start all over again with someone new. Better the devil you know…"

"Yeah, yeah, right." Tom had gone out, letting the door slam behind him.

****

The scene that greeted Madison at the small airport was one of organized chaos. Vehicles, emergency and otherwise, crowded the parking area, and on the runway two retardant bombers were being reloaded and refueled by men running like worker ants between them. With dense clouds of smoke hanging low in the dark sky, it resembled a war zone or a nightmare.

Madison parked as much out of the way as possible, locked the dogs inside with the windows cracked, and ran into the terminal building.

"Any word of Clay Archer?" she asked a burly grey-haired man behind the desk, who seemed to be at the hub of activities.

"You his wife, girlfriend, what?" He glanced up at her.

"A...friend."

"Yeah, well, no word yet. We're searching. You can take a seat if you like, and wait. Only keep out of the way. Andy!" He turned and bellowed to a man in coveralls rushing past him. "Why aren't those planes off the ground yet? Get a move on!"

Madison spotted a group of people dressed in orange jumpsuits with the words "Search and Rescue" on their backs gathered around a map on the far wall.

She joined them. "Are you searching for Clay Archer?"

"Yeah, but it's lookin' bad." A bearded man turned to face her. "Near as we can tell, his plane went down smack dab in the middle of that old firin' range. If the fire don't get him, one of those old shells explodin' from the heat probably will."

Madison took a seat on a bench by the wall. She knew she couldn't stay long, not with the dogs waiting in her vehicle. But just for a few minutes...

The phone on the coordinator's desk rang. He picked it up, listened.

"Yeah. Okay. Right away." He replaced the receiver, stood up, and bellowed, "Okay, guys. The order's come through. The town's got to be evacuated. Everyone except firefighting personnel is to leave the area immediately." He turned to Madison. "That means you, lady."

Chapter Fourteen

Clay Archer's chest ached, his throat burned, and his eyes felt like so much raw meat. But he was alive and had been able to half climb, half crawl out of his crashed plane. He'd stumbled away from it and into the bush mere seconds before it exploded into flames. Leaning against a giant pine, his heart banging at his ribs, he watched as his plane dissolved into a ball of fire in the shallows of the filthy lake where he'd ditched it.

Damn it, damn it, damn it!

Nausea overwhelmed him, and he vomited. As he wiped his mouth with the back of his hand, he was loath to believe what he was seeing. One of those formerly mythological toxic holding ponds lay in ugly reality right in front of him.

He rubbed his temples with filthy fingers in an effort to relieve the pounding of his head. *I have to get moving, have to try to walk out of here…before the fire catches up with me. I'll think about this later.* He dropped his hands and saw that one was wet and red. *Hell. A head wound. Just what I need.*

Doggedly he turned toward what he calculated was north and Chemsly. Stumbling from tree to tree for support, barely keeping himself on his feet, he began to walk.

****

Madison drove slowly up the winding backcountry

road through heavy smoke. She knew she should be on the highway headed away from Chemsly and the fire, but she couldn't leave. Not until she knew Clay was safe or…

She cut the second possibility from her mind and returned her attention to driving. With a lifelong knowledge of these backcountry roads, she was confident she could return to the highway in minutes, if necessary, by any one of a number of dirt or chip-sealed access roads. She kept her radio tuned in for the latest news on the fire and updated reports from the local EM station.

The road ended at an eight-foot-high gate that advised people not to go beyond that point because of the danger of unexploded ammunition. Her time in Africa had made her aware of the importance of such a warning.

When she reached the barrier with its large warning sign, she braked to a halt and got out. The air, thick with smoke, rushed into her nose and throat, chafing, making her cough.

She looked back down the road. Maybe this hadn't been such a good idea. The trail was pot-holed and narrow. Would she be able to return over it, even though she'd managed to get this far?

"Dr. Todd, I presume?"

She whirled.

Clay Archer, clothes torn and filthy, dried blood caked on the side of his head, appeared out of the smoke at the left side of the gate.

"Clay!" All the relief in her heart gushed out in the single word.

"Yeah, Clay Archer…in at least part of his flesh."

He forced a rueful grin.

"Let me help you." Heart pounding, she thrashed through the thicket beside the gate to get to him.

As she moved to put an arm about his waist, he captured her in one of his and pulled her to him. The next instant he was kissing her…kissing her until her head swam, her body turned molten, and she responded with every ounce of sensual energy she possessed. It didn't matter that he was filthy and wounded. He was alive.

"I had to do that." He quirked a corner of his mouth when he finally drew back. "A celebration of having survived. I'd appreciate it if you waited until I'm feeling a bit less wonky before you deck me."

"Did it seem as if decking you was on my mind?" She looked up at him and let a small grin curl her lips.

A big, cold drop of water struck her cheek, then another and another.

"Oh, my God, it's raining!" she gasped. And suddenly they were laughing, laughing like two lunatics and holding each other as if they'd never let go, as an all-out deluge burst over them.

"Come on!" she cried, pulling free and putting a supportive arm around his waist. "We've got to get moving! In a few minutes this road will turn into a river of muck. You need medical attention, and I've got two passengers waiting, one of which will definitely be very glad to see you."

****

"Madison, we have to talk. There's something I've discovered, something I have to tell you." Clay looked over at her as she struggled to keep her vehicle moving steadily through the mud, rain, and branches bedeviling the old road.

"Can't it wait? You sound as if every word you utter hurts. And I have to concentrate on my driving."

"I know, but I've got to tell you just one thing…Madison, I found one of those lethal ponds."

"You what!" Madison braked so abruptly the Jeep slid toward the trees. With a deft swing of the wheel, she got it back under control before she stopped the vehicle to stare at him. He grunted as pain lurched through him.

"I said I found one of those blasted ponds you've been raving about."

"Clay, that's wonderful!" Madison let the engine idle as she stared over at him. "Can you take me there? We'll need samples, photos…"

"Hold on." He suppressed a groan as he tried to make himself more comfortable in the small space of the passenger seat. "Until we've investigated it ourselves, we've got to keep it quiet. Having a stampede of curious citizens all over the place—not to mention the media—won't do us any good. Agreed?"

She hesitated.

"Agreed," she said finally, and eased her SUV back into motion. "How do we get there?"

"The plane I flew here from Alberta. I'll need to get an exact fix on the location before we try to approach by land. Maybe, in a couple of days, once the smoke has cleared…"

"And you've had a chance to recover," she said. "But why are you telling me? You could have remained quiet and kept me looking indefinitely."

"Because those toxic ponds exist and I'm responsible. Because I trusted a man I shouldn't have.

Because I should have investigated on my own."

He turned back to stare out the windshield into the bucketing rain. "Because, no matter what you think of me, I value life in all its forms and want to protect it."

They drove the rest of the way to the Chemsly Hospital in silence.

****

"How is he?" Madison got up from her chair in the emergency area waiting room as her mother came out of the doorway.

"As well as can be expected, considering what he's been through." Molly Todd smiled and touched her daughter reassuringly on the arm. "All he needed was a shoulder relocated and a few stitches to close the wound under his hairline. Of course, he's bruised and battered, but what he mostly needs are rest and lots of liquids. Steve has had him admitted overnight as a precautionary measure. There'll be more x-rays and tests in the morning before he's released."

"All good news." Madison gave her mother a quick hug, then turned and headed for the door. "Tell Clay I'll take care of Chance and that I'll pick him up when he's released."

"Madison, just a minute." Her mother, still in surgical scrubs, followed her. "What's going on between you and Clay? Pick him up when he's released? That hardly seems like the action of a woman who only yesterday went on television to make him look like a villain."

"It's complicated, very complicated, Mom." Madison met her mother's blue-eyed query head on. "But, rest assured, you'll be among the first to know if and when I get it sorted out."

She gave her mother a quick peck on the cheek and hurried out of the hospital.

****

"Madison, we need to talk." Clay Archer stood on her doorstep, dressed in jeans, plaid shirt, and cowboy boots, a ring of white bandage showing beneath his Stetson. Blue eyes bloodshot, he sported a dark stubble. And still looked way too damn sexy.

"Come in." Madison stepped aside. "You're limping."

"Yeah, guess I twisted a muscle or something," he said as he handled Chance's greeting. "Hello, guy. Good to see you, too."

"Sit." She indicated a chair near the fireplace in the small, neat living room.

"Thanks." He removed his hat and hung it on the rack by the door.

"Coffee?" she asked. "I just put on a fresh pot."

"No, thanks. A glass of ice water would be welcome."

"No problem."

When she returned with it, he was stretched out in the chair, his eyes closed. A gush of compassion washed over her. The plane crash had been traumatic enough. Finding those toxic ponds must have been like salt in the wound.

He drew himself up at her approach, flinched, and accepted the glass she'd filled with ice and water. He took a long drink.

"Thanks." He set it aside. "Can't seem to get enough of the stuff." He gave her a wry grin. "I must be getting old. Once upon a time I could land rough and never even get a headache. Now"—he leaned back in

179

the chair—"I hurt all over and feel as dried up as a raisin."

"I was going to pick you up at the hospital when you were released," she said. "Didn't my mother tell you?"

"She did, but I had things to do that couldn't wait. I hitched a ride to the airport, picked up my truck, and headed out to Tom's to check on the livestock."

"And?"

"They're all fine. Tom Mills is a good man, Madison." He looked over at her, and she caught the question in his words.

"Yes, he is." She met his gaze. "He's been my friend since I was in grade school."

"Nothing more?"

"At one point, in high school, yes."

"And now?"

"Friends. Look"—she got up and went to stand in front of him—"this is beginning to sound like twenty questions, none of them relevant to the problem at hand, namely those contaminated ponds you found in the bush."

"Oh, I think it's very relevant." He grimaced as he got up to face her. "Because we have to move our personal problems out of the way before we can get on with changing the world...or, at least, Chemsly."

"What personal problems?"

"Come on, Dr. Todd. You know exactly what I mean. We've got this hot chemistry going between us, and I don't just mean physical...although I'm not crazy enough to minimize that aspect."

"Okay, okay!" She put her hands on her hips and struggled to look annoyed. "But that's easily resolved.

We ignore it and move on."

"I don't think so." He spoke with slow deliberateness as he took her into his arms. "I really don't think so." His words became a sensuous mutter. A moment later he was kissing her until her senses swirled, until every inch of her body was responding, until she couldn't stop, wouldn't if she could.

When he pulled away, she stared up at him in astonishment.

"So much for that idea," she exhaled.

"So here's another." He held her out from him, the sincerity in those killer-blue eyes only making her want him more. "You tell me your story, all of it. Then I'll tell you mine. We've got to clear the air between us, Madison, because we might be headed into something serious."

"You think?"

"Yeah, I think. Don't you?"

She hesitated, then: "Yes," with an exasperated sigh of resignation.

"Scary, isn't it?" He grinned and reached out to run his knuckles gently down her cheek. "But you could sound just a tad enthusiastic."

"Sorry. It's only that it presents a whole lot of problems."

"Sure it does, but we're both fighters. We'll battle through it." He broke the spell by sitting down abruptly. "Damn, I'm weak as a kitten. Good time for making plans."

She hesitated, then with a little reluctant toss of her head sank onto the couch opposite him. "Okay. What do you suggest we do next?"

"Tomorrow we take a little trip in my plane and

ascertain the exact location of that pond. Most of the smoke from the fire will have cleared by then, and I should be able to get a fix on it. But don't tell anyone what we're up to. We don't know who we can trust."

He picked up his glass and took another drink of water. "Now, tell me about you and your committee and all you know about Rick Reid."

"Hmmm." Madison paused. "Well, Rick had a difficult childhood. His father lost his job at the mill because of a drinking problem, and his mother had to take work cleaning houses to feed Rick and his brothers and sister.

"Rick took a job with a Glendon Forest Products woods crew the minute he graduated from high school. By all accounts he was clever, hardworking, and ambitious. Within a few years he became a woods boss. A couple of years later, he moved into the mill as a shift boss. And so on and so on until he was general manager. Apparently Glendon Gregory recognized his abilities and utilized Rick to his advantage."

"Like he might have utilized a son," Clay muttered. "Sorry." He looked up at Madison and kinked a corner of his mouth. "Old resentments dying hard."

"You and your stepfather were never close, were you?"

"He couldn't stand the sight of me." Clay shrugged. "I think he was jealous that my mother might have cared more for me than him. Not important. I managed. Anything else I should know about Mr. Reid? Has he ever been married? Lived with someone? Is he currently involved in a serious relationship?"

"Not that I know of, although there have been rumors about him and his secretary. Why do you ask?"

"I'm trying to understand what would make a man attempt a cover-up of this size."

"And do you?"

"Partly, I think." He leaned back with a sigh. "What time can you be ready to take off tomorrow? I can have the plane ready at eleven a.m."

****

He'd kept stealing glances at her from the moment she'd climbed into the cockpit beside him and buckled herself in. Now, in the air at cruising altitude, he had to admit he was impressed. Not once had she shown any of the nervousness he'd usually witnessed with people unaccustomed to small planes. In fact, she seemed totally at ease.

"Do I have dirt on my face, or is there some other reason for all those furtive glances?" Her lips twitched upwards at the ends.

"They couldn't have been successfully furtive." He chuckled.

"Not even behind those fancy sunglasses," she replied. "So why?"

"Most people get a little uneasy the first time they go up in a small aircraft." He checked his heading before turning to her. "You appear as calm as a mountain lake."

"Maybe that's because this isn't my first time…or even my tenth."

"Is that a fact? May I ask where you got all this air time?"

"In Africa. I traveled to remote villages in a plane like this, along with the MD I worked with."

"Ah, ha! A grizzled kindly gentleman pushing sixty, happily married, with pictures of grandchildren always at the ready?"

"Hardly. Dr. Jason Kenny was thirty-six, single, and pretty darned attractive."

The moment the words were out of her mouth, her teeth clamped down on her lower lip.

"Can I take it, then, that you and this Dr. Kenny were more than co-workers?" *Damn, that sounded nosey and petty.*

"For a while." She took a pair of sunglasses from her jacket pocket, put them on, and swiveled to gaze out over the acres of fire-ravished forest ahead of them. Smoke still rose in lethargic puffs and columns from the smoldering devastation.

"But not anymore?" *Avoiding looking at me. Not good. And that attempt at a casual tone…yeah.*

"Definitely not anymore. He has someone else. Now can we end this inquisition and get on with the job we came to do?"

"Sure." He returned his attention to flying. He wasn't proud of the fact that he felt better. Madison had been hurt by this guy, seriously hurt, and he had no right to find relief, even pleasure, in it. But, man, he was glad the guy had fallen off the radar.

"Over this way, I think." He tried to distract himself by veering the plane to the right.

The contaminated pond loomed up in front of them. Previously hidden by the forest's canopy, after the defoliation of the fire it stood out like an ugly scar in the face of an already abused landscape.

She shoved her sunglasses onto the top of her head and put a camera to her eye. As they swooped lower over the pond, she started snapping.

"Can you swing over the pond again?" she asked

when they'd gone beyond it. "And this time lower."

"Hang on." He turned the Piper Cub and swooped down.

"Good enough?" he asked when they were beyond the pond and he nosed the plane back up into the sky.

"All I can do from here." She put the camera down and replaced her sunglasses. "Now I have to get down there and take samples."

"*I* have to get down there and take samples," he said, arcing the plane back toward the airport. "This mess belongs to me, remember?"

****

"We'll take your horses." Madison looked up at him as they paused between their vehicles in the airport parking lot.

"Horses?"

"It's a long hike to that pond, and we'll need to bring out both soil and water samples. I'll borrow a pack pony and horse trailer from Tommy. You get one of the mill trucks with a hitch and the power to pull it."

"Just a minute." She started to get into her Jeep, but he stopped her with a hand on her arm. "We can't borrow anything from Tom Mills. He'll want to know why, and until we know exactly what we're up against, the fewer people who know, the better."

She hesitated, then nodded. "Agreed. I'll tell him we're going on a little overnight trail ride."

"And have him slavering with jealousy? I don't think so. I don't need any more enemies than I already have in this town."

"Don't be ridiculous! Tommy's not like that. He knows there's never going to be anything more than friendship between us."

"Yeah, right."

"Don't judge every man by yourself, Clayton Archer. Some guys can actually be happy and contented to have a purely friendly, purely platonic relationship with…"

She couldn't finish. He'd caught her in his arms in the deserted parking lot and was kissing her. He hadn't planned to, knew it was probably the worst thing he could have done, given the location and the intensity of his feelings, but he couldn't help himself. There she stood looking up at him, green eyes bright with a sincerely innocent belief in her words, her lips soft and pink and inviting, and he'd lost it, his vows to wait until the mill fiasco was solved vanishing like so much snow in April sunshine.

And she was responding to him, letting him draw her full length against his body, melting into him.

"Ah, damn it, let's just go and get those horses!" He managed to back off with a supreme effort both mental and physical. "While I still can."

"Whatever you say." She stepped away from him, a coy smile tipping her lips. "Remember this state of our affair is your idea."

Chapter Fifteen

"Ready?" Clay Archer swung up into Scout's saddle and turned to Madison, mounted on Candy beside him.

"Ready." She touched her heels to the mare's sides and trotted off down the trail into the woods.

Clay took one last look at the securely locked 4x4 pickup and horse trailer in the clearing, adjusted the pack horse's lead rope in his gloved hand, and urged Scout after her. Tom's sturdy bay gelding, laden with camping gear and sample containers, trotted easily at the end of his tether.

He'd borrowed the animal and the trailer from the farrier on the pretext that he was going camping overnight alone. He'd told Tom his own mare Candy wasn't trained as a pack pony and that he wouldn't trust her on the trip. Tom had been quick to oblige. Clay hadn't been fooled by his alacrity. Tom Mills was most probably thinking that the expedition would take him away from Madison at least briefly. A wry grin twisted his mouth. What Tom Mills might do if he learned Madison was accompanying him could be a problem.

****

Clay caught up to her at the first bend in the trail. As it widened, he jogged his mount into position beside her. He copied her move as she slowed Candy to a walk.

187

"Better save the horsepower," she said. "This could be a rough ride. If I remember correctly, this trail crosses two streams and leads up a couple of pretty steep inclines. There are also a few swampy areas."

"But according to your map, it will take us within a ten-minute hike of the pond. That is, if we don't tread on any unexploded shells."

"Hey, are you chickening out?" She glanced at him from under the peak of her baseball cap. "If so, just hand over the pack pony and head back to town."

"Is that what you think of me? That I'd turn tail and leave you out here alone?" He adjusted his Stetson and avoided her eyes. "I know your experiences in Africa have probably familiarized you with unexploded shells and the like, but I can hack a bit of danger, too. Gets the adrenaline pumping. Probably good for my health. Get me back in shape."

"Fine. So we're both in for the long haul and out for the truth, okay?"

****

A half hour later, green trees and living undergrowth gave way to a landscape of devastation as they arrived at the beginning of the burn. For as far as they could see, the area had been ravaged and lay stark, charcoal grey, and lifeless. The spikes of the few trees that had remained standing stuck out like wizened, tortured fingers pointing accusingly upward at a sky that had released its rain too late for them. Beside the trail lay the half-burned corpses of a buck and doe.

"Overcome by smoke," Madison commented quickly, and Clay realized his expression must have reflected the nausea in his gut. "They didn't die of burns, Clay."

He nudged Scout on ahead. He couldn't look at the bodies any longer.

At noon they paused beside a brook amid the ashes, watered the horses, and ate a lunch in their saddles.

"Not much of a place for a picnic," he said as he leaned on the saddlehorn, a thick ham sandwich in his hand.

"Definitely not." Madison bit into an apple and chewed slowly. "I'll be glad when we reach that meadow the fire skipped...the one we saw from the plane...and set up camp. There appeared to be a good-sized brook running through it. The horses are filthy, and so are we. Maybe we can all get cleaned up, even if I'm not thrilled about using water so near that toxic mess."

"The brook's source, like this one, is back in the hills. I doubt it's contaminated." Clay removed his hat and rubbed his damp forehead with the back of his wrist. "Man, this is a warm day for October. Wish that brook was deep enough to do some serious skinny-dipping." He looked over at her and winked.

"We have an environmental mystery to solve before we consider anything like that." She clucked to Candy and headed off down the trail.

Clay slapped his hat back onto his head, wound the packhorse's lead around the saddlehorn, took a big bite out of his sandwich, and followed her.

He admired the auburn braid that hung down her back, the determined set of her shoulders, the way her shapely, jean-clad hips melded into the saddle. And, damn it, her teasing had the power to send all kinds of wild, erotic images racing through his mind. She sure knew how to lead a man on.

****

The small campfire on the bank of the brook crackled and snapped as Clay added more twigs and branches. In the cooling autumn twilight, Madison welcomed its warmth. Seated on her bedroll beside it, she drew up her knees, locked her arms around them, and gazed into the dancing flames.

"I've always loved camping," she said. "My dad and I used to go every year around this time."

She took a sip of wine from the tin cup in her hands. She'd been surprised when he produced the bottle, but hadn't protested sharing it with him.

"You and your father were close." He hunkered down beside her and replenished her drink. "You must miss him a lot."

"I do. But if you think my reasons for wanting pollution controls at your mill are purely personal…" Anger festered out of her emotions, and she found her tone resonating with it.

"Did I say that? Man, you're prickly on the subject. I was simply thinking how great that must have been. I never knew my biological father. He was killed when I was two, in an industrial accident at the steel mill where he worked. Defective machinery was suspected but never proven. Therefore, no insurance settlement for my mother and me." He paused and used a long stick to poke at the fire.

"Clay, I'm sorry. I had no idea…" His revelation brought her words out in a half-gasp.

"Yeah, well, it was a long time ago." He avoided her eyes and took a drink of wine. "But as I got older, it made me realize the importance of workplace safety."

"It must have been a horrible shock to your mother." Startled by his confession, she ignored his last sentence. "How old was she?"

"Twenty-one." The answer didn't quite accomplish the casual tone he seemed to have attempted. "Yes, it was. She and my father married on the day they graduated from high school, with nothing but love and both their families' disapproval, so when he was killed she had no one to run home to, no education that would help her support herself and her child."

He reached for the bottle and splashed more wine into his cup.

"Consequently she married Glendon Gregory." Madison believed she understood.

"Not right away." He drew up his knees and rested his arms on them, the tin mug clasped between his hands. "For a while she tried to make it on her own, waitressing, working as a salesgirl in department stores, housekeeping in hotels, that kind of stuff. She met my stepfather while she was cleaning his hotel room." Bitterness surfaced in his tone.

"You didn't like her choice."

"That's putting it mildly." A sneer curled his mouth at one corner. "He didn't want me from the get-go, and the feeling was reciprocated. Right after they were married, he started shipping me off to boarding schools and summer camps."

"Your mother didn't say anything, didn't try to stop him?" Madison's heart lurched as an image of a lonely little boy with blue eyes too large for his thin face standing with an oversized suitcase in his hand entered her imagination.

He shrugged. "Glendon Gregory held the purse

strings, and he was supporting us both a thousand times better than my mother alone ever could have. She believed those fancy schools were the best thing that could happen to me."

"Was it worth it?" Madison straightened up and turned to look at him. In the flickering firelight, his face was shadowed, difficult to read. "Surely you'd have been happier alone with your mother."

"Sure," he said softly. "But for years we both struggled along under the misapprehension that we were each doing it because it was best for the other. We never discussed it, until after my mother had a stroke and became dependent on a wheelchair for getting around, shortly before my graduation from university. It was then we discovered we'd each sacrificed the years we could have spent together for the security we thought we were procuring for the other."

"Oh, Clay, how tragic for you both!" Madison put a hand on his arm.

"Yeah, well, I guess there's a lesson in all this," he said, staring into the fire. "You can suffer a lot if you're not honest about your feelings. My mother and I were never great at baring our souls."

"But once you'd talked, discovered all you both really wanted was to be together…"

"It was too late. My mother couldn't walk, couldn't manage on her own. She needed constant, expensive care. Just out of university with no job, I wasn't in a position to provide it. Glendon Gregory was and, to his credit, did. I couldn't take her away from that kind of state-of-the-art situation until I had enough money to make her a comfortable life with me."

"Understandable." Madison rested her chin on her

drawn-up knees and gazed into the fire that was crumbling into embers. "So what did you do?"

"Since a business degree doesn't usually catapult you into a six-figure income overnight, I looked around to find a career that might. Alberta appeared to be the place where a man could make big money quickly. I headed out there. At first I worked on the oil rigs. And hated it. Finally one of the guys suggested I try ranch work. I'd told him I was a pretty fair rider…the fancy boarding schools Gregory shipped me off to mostly had excellent riding facilities and instructors. So I decided to give it a try, with the idea of earning enough to buy a place of my own and bringing my mother out to join me."

"Didn't work, huh?"

"I did get a job on one of the larger ranches, but I soon found out I had a lot to learn. Riding on English saddles and show jumping didn't much prepare me for the work, aside from the ability to stay on a horse. I loved the lifestyle, though, and held out the hope that, if I saved every cent, I could get a house for my mother and me."

"But you never succeeded." Madison caught him by the arm as he started to turn away. "Clay, what happened?"

"What happened?" He looked over at her, emotions clouding his eyes, crumpling the strong lines of his face. "Death happened. My mother died before I could afford to take her away from that mausoleum."

He lurched to his feet. Leaving her sitting alone by the embers of the campfire he strode off toward their supplies.

****

As he opened the insulated packsack and removed the wieners, Clay Archer couldn't believe what he'd just done. He'd told Madison Todd facts of his life he'd never divulged to another living soul.

He'd always prided himself on keeping his past and its pain locked away from the world. Suddenly, all it had taken was a couple of glasses of wine and the intimacy of a campfire with a beautiful, sympathetic woman to make him spill his guts. Not really such a tough nut to crack after all, was he.

He tried not to think about a future that could witness the mill's closure, a future where the Abby Archer Gregory Rehab Center might have to remain an unfulfilled dream.

But he wouldn't tell Madison that last part…at least not yet. He didn't want her becoming bogged down in feelings of mixed loyalty before she'd accomplished what she'd set out to do, until she was truly convinced she'd done all she could for the people of Chemsly and to get at least a bit of restitution for her father's death. Until she was free to come to him in a relationship untainted by regrets and recriminations.

****

"Listen." Madison, rolled up in her sleeping bag on the opposite side of the tent, drew his attention. "It's raining."

"Great. Nothing quite like the sound of rain on the roof to lull a person to sleep." Clay adjusted the jacket he was using as a pillow and stretched out with a contented sigh.

"I agree. A rainy night snug and warm inside a tent was always one of my favorite things about camping."

"Was?" He rolled on his side to face her in the

darkness.

"I haven't gone since Dad died."

"Well, if you enjoy it, we'll do it often...once we get this mess about the mill cleared up."

"You have high hopes, Mr. Archer." Madison snuggled down into her sleeping bag, ready to abandon the discussion.

"As a matter of fact, I have. After I talked to your mother and sister about our future..."

"You what!" Madison bolted up onto one elbow to glare over at his dark silhouette lying stretched out on his bedroll, hands clasped behind his head. "You talked to Mom and Paige about us? When? Where? Why?"

"Calm down." She heard a deep, throaty chuckle in his tone. "You sound like a newspaper reporter. I talked to your mother when I spent the night in the hospital after I crash-landed. I told her how you'd come to find me, the risks you took. I told her I admired your courage and determination. I told her..."

His voice trailed off.

"Told her what?" Madison felt hollow with apprehension.

"Well, it may have been a bit of the painkillers talking, but I told her I loved you."

"Oh, Clay, you didn't!"

"Cool down, Doctor. Those pills may have loosened my tongue, but I'm not sorry. I would have told her sooner or later."

"And what did she say?" Madison tried to breathe normally, fearing she might hyperventilate at any minute.

"She said she didn't know me well enough to have an opinion," he replied.

"Good. That's sensible, exactly what I would have expected from her."

"She also said…" He paused.

"Yes?"

"She also said we'd better clear up the problems between us before we got any more involved."

"So that's where your words of wisdom came from." She recalled his comments to her on his first day out of the hospital.

"Partly." He shifted on his bedroll. "But I guess I knew it even before your mother put it into words. I just wasn't ready to admit it."

"Okay, now tell me about Paige." Slightly relieved, Madison settled back on her sleeping bag. "Lord only knows what you said to her."

"Take it easy." Again she heard the deep, sensuous chuckle. "I met her at the supermarket when I was shopping for supplies to bring on this trip. Your sister is a pretty terrific gal who cares a great deal about you."

"What did she want you to do? Romance her one-track-minded sister into throwing in the towel?"

"She wants you to be happy, as happy as she is, that's all."

"Yes, yes, I know that." Madison eased back down on her bedroll. "I've put so many people in difficult positions. But I had to. You understand, don't you, especially now that you've found that toxic pond?"

"Yeah." The word was a tired exhale. "I do. Let's get some sleep, Madison. I'm bushed."

"Sure."

****

He heard her bubble mattress crinkle. A few minutes later her regular breathing told him she was asleep.

She was close to finding evidence that would prove her theories and vindicate her work. No wonder she could sleep quickly and peacefully. He, on the other hand, was still conjuring up probabilities—the probability that Rick Reid had bribed government officials to make his mill pass inspections, the probability that he'd used immigrant labor to build a pipe line to those toxic holding ponds…immigrant labor he could easily have coerced into working in hazardous conditions, silenced with the threat of deportation.

Clay rolled over and pounded the jacket he was using as a pillow. Damn Rick Reid. He had one hell of a lot of explaining to do.

****

Clay woke to the smell of coffee. He rolled over, stretched, and for a moment thought he was back at his old job at the ranch. Then he heard her humming softly and remembered exactly where he was and with whom. A slow grin spread across his face.

With a grunt he pulled himself to his feet and stretched again to relieve the stiffness sleeping on the ground had produced. Running a hand through his hair, he ducked out of the tent into morning sunlight.

"Good morning." He rested his hands on his hips and drew a deep breath of the crisp air. The acrid smell of burning had been lessened by the night's rain, and now clear skies and a light breeze had freshened the area.

"Good morning." She turned from where she was hunkered down beside a small camp stove and smiled up at him.

Without makeup, her hair gathered back into a braid, Madison Todd was so darned pretty she made him want to take her into his arms and kiss her until, if it would ever be possible, he was satisfied.

But that wouldn't be right. Not just yet.

"I smelled coffee," he said.

"You certainly did." She picked up a tin cup, filled it, and handed it to him. "Guaranteed it will knock your eyes open."

He took a sip and flinched.

"Too strong?"

"No, no, it's just fine." He reached for a packet of sugar from among the supplies she'd spread out on a blanket. *Man, this is bad stuff!*

"Clay." She turned to face him at eye level as he squatted down beside her to doctor his coffee. "There's something you should know about me."

"Yeah?" He squinted into the sun. He didn't like unpleasant surprises first thing in the morning.

"I'm not like Paige and my mother," she said turning away to pour herself a cup of coffee.

"And that means?"

"Clay, I can't cook!" She turned back to him, distress widening her eyes. "Didn't you realize that on Thanksgiving, when they were both so anxious to keep me out of the kitchen?"

For a moment he stared at her before he burst out laughing.

"Well, honey, that's perfectly okay." He chuckled. "Because I can. I'll get eggs and bread and whip us up some of the best French toast you'll ever eat."

The relief mirrored in her face made him chuckle again as he reached for the skillet. But as he opened the bread bag, he paused.

"What about that quiche you served when we had breakfast out at the estate? As I recall, it was pretty darn good."

"Think. Remember I told you I bought it?" She glanced over at him through lowered eyelashes. "I just heated it up. Ditto for the coffee. It came in a thermos. Sorry to disillusion you. But then I guess it isn't the first time, is it?"

"Madison, anything you did was for what you saw as a good cause." He looked squarely into regretful green eyes. "I wish I could say the same about Rick Reid." He picked up a stainless steel bowl and cracked an egg against its rim.

"Clay, wait." She stilled his hands. "I told you Rick grew up in poverty. He knows what a man's losing his job at the mill can do to a family. He wasn't about to let that happen to people he'd known all his life. I'm not saying what he did was right, and Lord knows we've fought some bitter battles, Rick and I, but I think you should at least try to look at the situation from his point of view."

"Nobody is ever a complete villain, right?" He stopped his assault on the eggs and turned back to face her.

"That's right." She smiled, and his heart flipped.

If he could someday have Madison Todd as his partner, he'd be one happy man.

Chapter Sixteen

Rick Reid swung from staring out the window into a dull red sun rising over the lifeless mill stacks as Clay entered his office.

"So she got what she wanted." He faced Glendon Forest Products' CEO, a glass with an inch of amber liquid covering its bottom in his hand. "Dr. Todd nailed us to the wall, and you helped her do it. Damn, I thought you had a whole lot more woman-savvy! I'm disappointed in you, Boss, really disappointed."

"Evidence can't be denied." Clay fought to control anger he knew would only prove counterproductive in the circumstances. "That's got nothing to do with Madison's getting what she wanted."

"Yeah, well, you said you found that pond when you crashed during the fire. You could have kept quiet about it. We could have cleaned it up on the QT. No one had to be any the wiser. Maybe if you hadn't had the hots for our local vet, you wouldn't have been all that eager to go on an overnighter with her, looking for pollution."

"It wasn't like that." Clay's control slipped notch by notch by notch.

"No? I suppose you think Miss Madison, with her fresh little girl-next-door looks, isn't capable of usin' people, men in particular? Well, let me fill you in on a bit of her romantic past."

"Dr. Todd's personal life has no place in this discussion." Madison's description of Reid's history and concern for the people of the town dissipated in a wave of anger.

He swung and headed for the door, but the mill manager was quicker. He crossed the room in long strides and placed his back against the door before Clay could reach it.

"Listen to me, Clay. You've got to know the truth about her before you go makin' one huge mistake. After you've heard what I have to say, if you feel the need, you can deck me a good one right on the jaw. Agreed?"

Clay hesitated.

"Come on, come on. What have you got to lose? Five minutes at the most."

He didn't want to listen, didn't want to agree to listen, but memories of his first impression of Madison flooded back into his mind—too good to be unattached. And then there'd been Tom Mills, and Dr. Jason Kenny, and...

"Talk," he said, anger and jealousy a revolting mixture in his gut.

"Well, then." Rick Reid heaved a sigh. "Let's sit."

"I'd rather stand."

"Suit yourself." The mill manager moved away from the door and headed for the bar. "Scotch?" he asked picking up a bottle.

"Just get on with it."

"Fine." Rick Reid added ice from a silver bucket to his glass. "This has been one hell of a week." He took a sip, bared his teeth, and drew a deep breath. "Nothin' quite like twelve-year-old Scotch. I'm gonna miss it."

"No one asked you to resign." Clay faced him

squarely. "You made a bunch of mistakes, but Madison has convinced me they were in a good cause. You wanted to keep the mill open for the town's sake. I can speculate that my miser of a stepfather refused to give you sufficient funds to modernize and cut the emissions. Given those facts, I see no reason to ask for your resignation."

"After the press gets finished crucifyin' me, I doubt I'll be able to find work in South America. Discovery of those holdin' ponds has created a field day for the media." He took another drink, then continued slowly, "Did you know Maddy and I were an item for a while right after she came back from Africa?"

The man's half drunk. And out to sucker-punch me. No point in disputing anything with him until he sobers up. But he and Madison...hell and damnation!

For a while I really thought we had somethin', you know?" He rounded his desk and sank into the big chair behind it. "Oh, sure, she was a doctor and I was only a guy who'd worked his way up from a woods hand, but, seein' who her sister had married, I thought I had a chance."

He paused and shook his head ruefully. "One Saturday, when these administrative offices were supposed to be closed, I came back to pick up some papers and found her goin' through my files. Somehow, sometime durin' our so-called relationship, she'd lifted my keys, had copies made, and found the security code in my wallet."

He quaffed the rest of his drink before rounding on Clay, bloodshot eyes burning with anger. "That'll give you a pretty good idea of how Dr. Madison Todd operates...if you'll forgive the pun or whatever it's called."

"You're lying!" Boiling, sickening anger rushed over him.

"Yeah? Ask her. Ask Jordan. How do you think I convinced him to testify at that meeting? I told him if he didn't I'd have charges of break-and-enter laid against his sweet little sister-in-law. I have her on security camera openin' my filing cabinet, tryin' to access my computer documents. Given that kind of evidence, Jordan caved."

Clay sucked in a deep breath through bared teeth and battled the urge to throttle Rick Reid on the spot. The fact that it would accomplish nothing was the only reason he could find.

Worst of all, some of what he was saying was hitting home. When he thought about it, Madison could have used him to get the evidence she needed to shut down the mill. Maybe she was getting ready to discard him like just another cardboard coffee cup. Like Rick Reid, like Tom Mills. Maybe even Dr. Jason Kenny.

"I'll be back."

He swung around and strode out of the office, not sure if it was heartburn or something as ridiculous as heartbreak that was tearing up his chest.

****

"Hello." He stood as Madison stepped out of her surgery into her deserted waiting room.

"Hello," she said, confused by the change in his demeanor. "Clay, is something wrong?"

"Oh, yeah. That is, if discovering the woman I was getting damn serious about has been using me."

For a moment she could only stare up into those intense blue eyes, now holding all the warmth of sapphire ice.

"At first, yes, but not later…I told you…" She finally managed to stammer out a reply. She had to be honest. "Clay…"

"Never mind 'later.' Let's go back to before all that." He crossed the room to stand close in front of her, and she imagined she could feel the heat of the anger emanating from his body. "Before, to Tom Mills and Dr. Jason Kenny and"—he paused, glaring at her with such passion she had to struggle not to step away from him—"back to Rick Reid."

"Rick was a mistake." Her heart skipped a beat. She should have told him. "I'm not proud of what I did, but Dad had just died, and I was willing to do anything…"

"Anything? Like sleeping with the mill manager?"

"No! What do you think I am? What did he tell you?" With nausea welling up inside, she realized where he'd gotten his information. "We dated a few times, he drank too much on a few occasions, and..."

"And you took advantage of those 'few occasions' to steal his keys and rifle his wallet. Nice."

He turned and strode out of the office, slamming the door behind him.

****

He adjusted his sunglasses, checked the instrument panel, and glanced back at Chance buckled into his seat behind him.

"Ready, buddy?"

The little dog glanced out the window and whined.

"Yeah, I know. Leavin' 'em isn't easy. But better now than later. I'm sorry you got involved with Ceilidh, but somewhere in Alberta there has to be another cute little bitch. I know there's Lacey Trent, who's a whole lot of fun and one heck of a looker, and who shoots straight from the hip."

He'd closed up the estate and taken the horses and cats to Tom Mills' place to board. And it hadn't taken all that long to set up renovations for the mill. A national company certified in pollution control had moved in to clean up the mess both at the facility and in the ponds back in the bush. Within a few months, Glendon Gregory Forest Products would once more be up and running, only this time safely. He'd come back from time to time to check on progress, but other than that there was nothing to keep him in Chemsly any longer.

Air traffic control gave him the all-clear, and he swung back into position.

"Up, up, and away," he muttered as he throttled up and headed down the runway.

But as the Piper Cub lifted off and nosed up and westward into the overcast sky, his usual feeling of euphoria didn't happen. Madison Todd's image flashed in front of him, and he wondered if he'd ever really feel good again.

Damn it. Ever since Thanksgiving he'd been having fantasies of him and Madison and a couple of kids…the kind of family he'd always wanted to be part of, with a grandmother like Molly and a sister-in-law like Paige and a brother-in-law like Jordan and a niece and nephew like Katie and Daniel, all getting together for holidays.

Rick Reid's stories and Madison's admission had torn that dream to shreds. He arched tired shoulders and tried to shove it all out of his mind. Maybe he wasn't meant to have an old-fashioned family life. Maybe Glendon Forest Products and its renovations were meant to occupy his time and energy. And a good-timin' Alberta cowgirl named Lacey Trent.

****

The mill had been closed for a month. Looking downriver at its impotent stacks, Madison experienced none of the elation she'd once believed she would. A good portion of the town's breadwinners were unemployed, including her brother-in-law, and an overwhelming feeling of having lost something integral to her own personal happiness had taken away the possibility of any exultation at her success.

She knelt and gathered Ceilidh into her arms.

"I wish there'd been some other way," she murmured. "I wish no one had to lose a job. I wish I'd told Clay about Rick. I wish…"

She buried her face in the little dog's ruff and vowed not to wish for any more impossibilities.

****

The announcement came a week before Christmas. The mill was going to undergo a complete refit to minimize its emissions. State-of-the-art technology would be installed starting immediately, and most of the laid-off workers would be recalled to do it. The remainder would return to work in the spring when renovations were due to be completed.

A huge party sponsored by Glendon Forest Products was to be held in the high school gymnasium to mark the occasion.

****

Madison swung right, then left, then all the way around in front of the cheval mirror in her bedroom.

She knew the little black dress and strappy high-heeled sandals were cliché, but she also knew she looked good in them.

With a sinking feeling, she thought about Clay Archer. He'd be there, all dark curly-haired handsome six-feet-plus of him, with that killer blue-eyed grin. At least indoors he wouldn't be wearing a Stetson, but those cowboy boots were pretty much ubiquitous with him. She'd just have to ignore his feet. But maybe he wouldn't ignore hers. She did have nice ankles.

"Do you think he'll notice, Ceil?" She turned to the little dog sitting on her bed. "Wouldn't you like to see Chance again?"

Ceilidh gave a sharp little bark and looked up at her, eyes bright and eager.

"Sorry, girl." Madison gave her a hug. "I shouldn't have raised your hopes for something that's not going to happen."

****

In spite of the subzero temperatures of the December night, the gymnasium was crowded. One of the biggest fully trimmed Christmas trees Madison had ever seen had been set up in a corner of the room, and Christmas songs from the sound system filled the air. Along one side, a buffet table that stretched the entire length of the room was loaded with food, and coffee, tea, and soft drinks were provided at each end. There was an open bar in a far corner. It looked as if nearly everyone in Chemsly had turned out for the event. Everyone from the town and more, she corrected herself, as she saw him and her heart skipped a beat.

Standing near the head of the buffet table, a coffee cup in one hand, Clay Archer wore a neatly pressed light blue shirt, jeans that appeared fresh and new, a wide leather belt with a silver buckle, and cowboy boots that looked like those she'd seen online featured on exclusive retail sites that catered to affluent westerners.

Beside him stood a tall, statuesque brunette, blue-black hair cascading down her back in a shining, straight cascade. High cheekbones and brown eyes completed this woman's earthy, exotic appeal. Dressed in a designer denim jacket trimmed with silver and jeans that looked tailor made, she caught the attention of every man who passed her way.

Madison's hopes plummeted. The woman was all-out gorgeous, the type to melt a man with a sly smile and send his hormones raging with a brush of a hand.

Damn you, Clay Archer. I bet she isn't even a friend. I bet she's someone you hired just to infuriate me.

As quickly as the thought occurred she recognized it for its craziness. The sheer petty deviousness of such a plan was nowhere near anything Clay Archer would do. Anyhow, as angry at her as he'd been when he left, he wouldn't have wasted time concocting such a scheme. In his eyes, she wouldn't have been worth the effort…petty thief, seducer for personal gain that he believed her to be.

Well, what the hell. Nothing left to lose.

Summoning her courage, she walked across the room with as much grace as feet and legs unaccustomed to six-inch heels would allow.

"Merry Christmas, Clay." She startled him. He'd been deep in conversation with his companion.

"Madison, hello. The same to you." He turned to

face her, surprise in his voice and expression. His gaze swept over her. "You look…great."

"Thanks. So do you. Did you arrive today?"

Town gossip had already informed her that he had, but she was aiming for light, innocuous conversation.

"Yeah, late this afternoon." He put an arm about the brunette's waist and drew her forward. "Madison, this is Lacey Trent. Her father owns the ranch where I work. Lacey, this is Dr. Madison Todd, the veterinarian I told you about."

"Nice to meet you, Doctor. Clay told me how you saved Chance's life. Good for you. I don't have to tell you how much that dog means to him."

"Nice to meet you, too, Miss Trent." Encouraged, she continued the conversation. "How is Chance?"

"Good…fine…well. Ceilidh?" Clay stumbled out the words.

"The same. She misses him."

Good Lord, why had she said that? The suggestiveness of her words brought on a gush of embarrassment. If she hadn't been wearing those ridiculous shoes she'd have turned and run.

"You'll be staying in Chemsly for a while?" Madison tried again for casual conversation.

"A few days. I only came down to take a quick look at the actual site. The work crew is doing a great job. I've been down to Tom's to check on my horses and the cats. Those kittens surely have grown. He tells me I'm good to leave them with him as long as I want."

"Wonderful." Madison forced a smile but felt her heart drop as a sick feeling gushed over her. He was going back to Alberta with *her*.

There was only one thing left to do. She turned to

his companion, that painful, phony smile in place.

"I hope your stay is a pleasant one, Miss Trent. Nice to see you again, Clay."

Mustering her dignity, she turned and started across the room just as the DJ cranked up the first tune designated to start the dancing. People flooded onto the floor. Someone in their haste to get to its center jolted her.

It was too much for those ridiculous heels. Madison lost her balance and would have toppled if strong arms hadn't caught her.

"Hey, Maddy, where are you going in such a hurry?" Tom Mills held her on her feet and grinned down at her. "Wow! Aren't you the hottest critter here tonight! Dance with me, pretty lady, and make every guy in the room jealous."

As she slipped into his familiar arms to the strains of "Moon River," she glanced over his shoulder and saw her mother moving onto the floor with Dr. Steven McLean, beside Paige and Jordan. Beyond them, Lacey Trent had slipped her arms about Clay Archer's neck and moved shapely hips in time to the music as she drew him in among the dancers.

So it was all working out. Everyone had someone. The mill was going to be repaired, and last week she'd heard that a much-needed state-of-the-art rehab center was to be built in memory of Clay's mother. It should have marked an ending as cliché as her outfit and as happy as the season was meant to be.

But it wasn't. Not for Dr. Madison Todd.

The song ended, and the DJ put on one with a fast, catchy beat, one to which Madison and Tom had loved to dance in their high school days.

"Ah, Maddy, they're playing our song!" Tom swung her about before she had time to protest. She looked into his laughing brown eyes. The years fell away and they were back in the high school gym, making everyone clear the floor and stand back to clap their hands and watch them go.

It was *déjà vu*. The crowd parted and let the dancers have center stage. Swinging her about, leading her in their familiar fancy moves, Tom brought her back to those happy times. When she looked into his grinning face, she had to smile. They were having fun, real fun, like when they went riding together or swimming or anything else. Her feet were actually behaving despite the ridiculous shoes. Clay Archer and his fancy girlfriend be damned. This was great.

When the dance ended to a rain of applause, she fell laughingly, gratefully, into Tom's arms for a waltz.

"That was great, Maddy." He grinned, his face damp. "But, man, it makes a guy realize he's getting on in years. I used to be able to dance a dozen of those without breaking a sweat."

"Not a dozen, Tommy." She chuckled. "But a goodly few."

"But look at you, Maddy. Still as cool as a cucumber...whatever that means. Maddy..."

"No, Tommy." She stopped him as she saw the seriousness coming back into his tone and expression. "We're old news, remember?"

"Sure, okay, but you can't blame a man for trying...especially with you looking the way you do tonight."

Her heart lurched as she saw the longing and disappointment in his eyes. Tom Mills was a good man, but she loved him only as a friend, and that was all it would ever be.

"Good evening." As the dance ended, Clay Archer had mounted the stage at the end of the gym and spoke. "Thank you all for coming. I hope you're enjoying yourselves."

An enthusiastic applause broke over the crowd.

"Good, very good. Well, then, I'm sure you're all aware by now of the plans for the mill's future. When it reopens in the spring, it will be a prime example of pollution control and appreciation of environmental concerns. At this point, I believe it's time we gave a round of applause to the lady and her committee largely responsible for these changes. Dr. Madison Todd, will you come forward, please?"

For a moment Madison could only stand staring until Tom's hand went to the small of her back, propelling her to the stage and up the first steps.

"Go on, Maddy. Take credit for all your hard work," he hissed, and she had no choice but to continue onto the stage.

"A nice round of applause for Dr. Madison Todd." Clay advanced across the stage to take her hand and guide her to its center. The audience responded with a thunderous outburst, but she barely heard. Electricity had raced through her body from the point of contact with the man just as it had on that stormy night in the old mansion.

"Thank you," she managed to say. "But the credit really goes to my committee and to Mr. Archer."

Feeling as if her face would burst into flame at any moment, Madison forced a smile and nod before retreating to the gym floor.

Why did he have to touch me? Why? Why? Dear God, just let me get out of here!

She headed out of the room and down the hall toward the foyer, where coats and boots waited for their owners.

"Madison!" His voice made her break into a half run as she realized he was following her. One shoe slipped. She kicked it off, pulled the other free, and continued to flee barefooted, clutching one shoe in her hand.

"Madison!" He caught up to her as she grabbed her coat from its peg and tried to force her feet into winter boots. "Madison, wait." He put a restraining hand on her arm. "We have to talk."

"What can there be to say, Clay?" Alone with him in the deserted foyer, Madison looked up at him, eyes swimming. "You don't trust me, and you've moved on. Lacey Trent is a beautiful woman. I thank you for the mill renovations, I truly do, but that ends whatever relationship we had. Goodbye, Mr. Archer. I wish you well."

She shoved her feet into her boots, pulled on her coat, and, grasping her single shoe, strode away from him, heart and soul aching.

****

"Rick." Clay stepped into the coffee shop beside Madison's office the following morning.

His former mill manager turned apprehensively from where he'd been buying coffee at the counter.

"Clay." He looked bad, hungover and bone weary, a two-day stubble covering his chin and jaws.

"I need to talk to you." Clay indicated a table and a pair of chairs near the window.

213

"Okay." Rick paused, looked at him, then picked up his cup and headed toward them. Clay purchased a decaf and followed him.

"Decaf?" Rick broke the tension as Clay sat down across from him. "What's up? Never heard of a cowboy who didn't want his java straight up and strong."

"Heartburn. Have it a lot lately."

"Heartache, more like. Listen, Clay, about Madison…" He leaned across the table toward him and lowered his voice.

"I don't want to talk about Madison Todd. I came here to talk about you. I want you back on the job, overseeing the refit, then as manager when the mill reopens."

Rick Reid stared him.

"Hell, man, are you sure?" His response was slow, suspicious. "After all that's happened?" He looked down into his coffee, his jaw working with a tic.

"You made mistakes, some of which were forced on you by my stepfather's penny-pinching. Others were in pursuit of what you believed integral to the town's employment situation and well being. None of it benefited you personally. I've had Paige Anderson going over the books, and she tells me that aside from those forgivable *faux pas* the mill has been one efficient and well managed business."

"Hell and high water, you hired Paige? You do know she's Madison's sister?"

"Of course I do. I believe in her honesty just as I believe in yours. With the improvements I've authorized, and a free hand, you're the best man for the job. What do you say?"

"Hell, yes! Thanks, man!" Rick jumped to his feet,

214

slopping coffee onto the plastic surface of the small table between them with the jostling it received. "Deal!" His hand shot out, and he stood, eyes bright.

Clay got up more carefully and accepted it.

"This is great!" Rick sat down again, and Clay followed his example. Rick's gaze dropped to his coffee, and his words softened. "I can't thank you enough, Clay. I've been helpin' my mother put my kid sister through college and wantin' to get serious with Chrissy. Not that the last bit has much of a chance of workin' out."

His hands gripping his cardboard cup, he looked over at Clay. "Now let me do something for you. Let me tell you the truth about Madison."

"No!" Clay bolted to his feet. "That's over. Closed book. Just forget it. Can you be back on the job tomorrow morning? I have to head back to Alberta, and I want us to have a meeting before I leave."

"Sure, sure." He gulped the rest of his coffee and stood. "I'll go home, get cleaned up, and head out there right now to take a look-see. But about Madison…"

"Rick, respect me on this one. I said forget it, and I mean it. I've got to go. I'm meeting Paige in a half hour." He headed for the door, then paused to turn back and say, "Good luck with Chrissy."

Chapter Seventeen

Madison stopped her small vehicle in front of the indoor arena that adjoined Tom's stable and climbed out. It was the middle of January, and she hadn't seen the farrier since Christmas Eve, when he'd stopped by her mother's (on Molly's invitation) for a cup of eggnog. Not hearing from him for nearly three weeks was a record, and she'd been growing concerned. When she passed his farm on her way to a call that morning, she'd decided to drop in on her return trip.

Wondering if he'd have time to have a short dressage session with her and Lady, the black horse she usually rode, she walked briskly over the snow-packed drive and past an unfamiliar 4x4 to the arena door. A customer or student, she mentally explained the vehicle as she shoved the panel inward.

It took her eyes a few moments to accustom to the indoor gloom after the brilliance of the sunny, snow-crusted morning. At first she saw only the outlines of two people on horses doing dressage exercises in the center of the ring. But as they came into focus she inhaled sharply.

Lacey Trent, mounted on Lady, was partnering Tom in the careful movements as he kept his big light grey in sync.

"Maddy, hi!" Tom saw her and broke off the exercise to lope over to greet her. "Just in time to give us your expert opinion of our performance. Lacey and I are considering competing in the Atlantic Winter Fair next month."

"Really?"

"Yeah, you remember Lacey Trent. She came east with Clay for the mill announcement. She and I got together after you left that party he threw before Christmas. We kind of hit it off, and I invited her to come back for a visit." His voice trailed off, a shy, embarrassed grin crossing his face. "Hope you don't mind."

"Tommy, of course not." Although a sense of loss fluttered through her, Madison smiled. "You deserve someone special. Lacey Trent appears she might just be that."

"She surely can handle a horse. Been riding since before she could walk." With a pleased softening of his features, he turned to look at the woman cantering smoothly around the arena.

"Very nice." Madison returned the woman's waved greeting. "I won't keep you from your practice. I haven't seen you for a while and wondered if you were okay. Obviously you are. Now I've got patients to see."

Altruism fading, she swung away and strode outside. Tommy had always been there for her, but she loved Clay. Now that woman had taken away both of the men she cared about.

"Maddy, wait!" Tom dismounted and strode after her. "Hold on just a minute!"

He caught up with her as she was about to get into her Jeep.

"Maddy, don't leave. Not like this. Let me explain."

"There's nothing to explain. You and Lacey obviously have a great deal in common. I wish you well."

"It wouldn't have happened if I'd thought there'd ever be a chance in hell for you and me, Maddy." His eyes begged her to understand, his breath forming a thin fog between them in the frosty air. "But after I saw how you looked when I told you his plane had gone down, I knew…"

"Well, you knew wrong. Clay Archer means nothing to me, absolutely nothing. Now move aside. I have patients to tend."

"Want to see the cat and kittens? They're doing real good."

"Not now. Some other time."

"He named the mother cat Patience."

"What?" She swung back.

"I said he named the mother cat Patience, maybe because he's being patient waiting for you to recognize the truth? Just thought you should know. But if you're really not interested…"

With a shrug, he opened the Jeep door.

"I'm not."

"Yeah, right." He stood back to let her get in, his tone reflecting his disbelief. "You're not fooling me. Call him, Maddy."

"I will…when hell gets as cold as today."

As she drove back toward her office, tears trickled down her cheeks. Not for Tom Mills. No, she was comfortable with the fact that he'd found someone who shared his interests. Her tears were for the memories his reference to Clay Archer had aroused. Even with Lacey Trent out of his life, he'd never come back to her. Not after Rick Reid's stories and innuendoes. Not after how she'd used him.

Call him. Right! As if he'd want to hear from me.

****

Clay shoved his reading glasses up onto the top of his head, leaned back in the swivel chair behind his desk, and looked out the window of his office at the Trent ranch. Dark and cold, the spring night was spitting a few flakes of snow among the freezing rain pellets that were turning the pens beyond the barns to mud. Already cows were beginning to calve. Born into this weather, the little guys had to be tough to survive. Tough like Dr. Madison Todd, ready to do anything to get her way.

Damn it, why does that woman always come back to haunt me? She's a manipulating little witch who's left a string of men lusting after her. The fewer times I have to encounter her, the better. Why I went running after her that night of the Christmas party I'll never know. Hormones must have been out of whack.

"Clay." Jim Trent strode into the office and sank down with a sigh onto the couch in front of the fireplace across the room. "Fire feels good tonight." He held out big, powerful hands to its warmth. "How's that inventory going?"

"Good, Jim. I'll have everything ready for tax season." Mentally Clay shook himself out of his reflections and flashed his employer a grin. "No worries."

"Fine, good to hear." Jim Trent stretched broad shoulders and looked over at his foreman. "I knew I did a smart thing when I hired a fella who not only knew his way around horses but had a business degree as well. What with me being away a fair bit, and Lacey, even with the same college education you have, not inclined to take things on, at least not yet, you've been pretty much of a blessing to me, young fella."

"You gave me a chance when I needed it." Clay stood and headed for the bar in the corner. "I'm glad I can help now." He turned to Jim Trent, held up the whiskey decanter, and raised an eyebrow in question.

"Sure, sure. This kind of night requires, as a Scotsman would say, a wee dram."

Clay dropped ice from a bucket into two glasses, poured a healthy measure into both, handed one to his employer, and took a seat in a leather chair opposite him by the fire.

"Lacey got back this afternoon." Jim Trent settled himself comfortably. "She's been running down to New Brunswick more times than I can count since she met that Tom Mills fella. I might just have to take a turn down there myself to meet the lad and find out exactly what his intentions are."

"He's a good man." Clay had to be honest about Madison's ex. "He owns a stable of fine horses, cares about animal welfare, and is an excellent farrier. On top of all that, he's a gentleman. Lacy could do a whole lot worse."

"Good with horses, eh? Well, maybe if this thing with my daughter continues, I'll have to approach the lad about relocating to Alberta. What do you think?"

"I think, provided he could bring his stock with him, Tom Mills might welcome a change of scene."

Why do I feel good about saying that and yet half-assed guilty? Even with Tom Mills out of the picture, I won't be going back to Dr. Madison Todd and her two-

faced ways.

"And what about you, young fella? How about coming down to New Brunswick with me? You could introduce me around...maybe even to that Dr. Todd Lacey tells me you have an eye for."

"Over and done, Jim. Something that will never work out. You go on down to the Maritimes. I'll look after things here."

****

Clay awoke to the ringing of his phone. As he struggled up on one elbow, he glanced at the lighted face of his clock radio. Three a.m.

"Yeah?" His voice was gruff from sleep.

"Clay, is that you?" Tom Mills' response brought him wide awake.

"Yeah...yes. Tom? What's wrong?"

"It's Maddy, Clay. She was helping one of my mare's foal, and..."

"And? And what? Jesus, Tom...!" He swung his feet onto the floor, a sick feeling in his stomach, his heart thudding.

"She got kicked, Clay. Pretty bad. The paramedics think a few broken ribs, a collapsed lung, maybe more. She's in surgery right now."

"I'm on my way." Clay dropped the phone, snapped on a light, and bolted for the closet.

"Come on, boy," he called to Chance. The Border Collie was stretching himself awake on the end of Clay's bed. "We're taking off for Chemsly, pronto."

****

Complications at the Toronto airport delayed him on a refueling stop, and it was late morning before he and Chance lifted off, late afternoon by the time he

221

reached Chemsly. Anxiety ripping at his gut, he left Chance in the care of an airport employee he'd gotten to know during his time in the town and caught a cab.

"I'll give you a hundred if you get me to the hospital in under ten minutes," he told the driver. "Damn the speed limits."

"You got it, man. Hang on."

****

At the hospital he found Molly, Paige, and Tom in the waiting room of the intensive care unit.

"How is she?" he asked, sweeping off his Stetson.

"We don't know yet. They had to operate again after I called you," Tom said, his face sallow and grim. His hand holding a Styrofoam coffee cup shook. "More problems with her breathing."

"Thank you for coming, Clay." Deathly pale, her eyes dark-rimmed, Molly looked up at him and offered a bleak smile. Paige, white-faced and grim, sat beside her mother, an arm draped about her sagging shoulders.

"Molly." Clay dropped on one knee in front of her. "Tell me what to do. Can money help? An airlift to a bigger hospital with more facilities, specialists?"

"Thank you, dear." Molly patted his hand, her eyes swimming. "Dr. McLean will do just fine."

"If you're sure." He got to his feet and looked down at Paige. "Jordan?"

"With the children. We didn't tell them about Madison. We're keeping them home from school today so no one else will. We'll explain it all…later."

"That's best. Is there anything I can do?"

"If you wouldn't mind going to the cafeteria and getting some chicken soup, maybe a couple of dinner rolls and a few crackers. She"—Paige's face furrowed as she glanced at her mother—"hasn't eaten since yesterday."

"Sure." Clay started off.

"I'll come with you." Tom followed him.

****

Fifteen minutes later, they left Paige trying to urge Molly to eat some of the food they'd brought from the cafeteria, while Clay and Tom took a walk out to the parking lot at Tom's suggestion.

"I need to move around," the farrier explained. "I was getting twitchy, too twitchy to be any good to Molly or Paige. As soon as we're sure Maddy's okay, I'll head back to Paige's and take over from Jordan. He should be with his wife. Katie and Daniel will perk me up, no problem."

"I can go." Clay was quick to volunteer. "I'm a responsible babysitter. I know Madison would like to see you if…when she wakes up."

"Wrong." They'd reached Tom's pickup. The farrier paused to lean against its muddy tailgate. "She'll want to see you."

"Yeah, right." He looked down at the toe of his boots.

"Yeah, right. Listen, man, you two love each other, and it's time you admitted it and started acting sensible. You both set out to avenge your parent's deaths, and you've done it. The mill's been renovated and, from what I've heard, plans are well underway for the rehab center. Now get on with your lives…together."

"I'm not trying to avenge…"

"Sure you are…by spending every cent of old Gregory's hoarded money to build that fancy recovery center. Think about it. You're avenging your mother's passing just as much as Maddy was looking for revenge by fighting to close the mill she blamed for her father's death. Clay, it's time to move on, to do the next right thing."

"Which, in your opinion, is?"

"Ask the woman to marry you."

"She wouldn't even consider it." He looked off into the foggy April afternoon. "And there are other considerations. No, it isn't in the cards, my friend."

"I didn't think Lacey'd agree to marry me, either, but she said yes. Now I guess I have to make a trip to Alberta to ask her father's permission…and see if he's willing to offer me a job on his ranch."

"Hey, that's great! Congratulations!" Clay offered his hand, and when Tom accepted it, clasped it in a firm grip. "You won't have any problems with Jim Trent. Whatever his only child and darling daughter wants, she gets. Apparently, for some strange reason, she wants you." He grinned.

"You think? Damn, I sure hope so."

"I'm happy for you, man. I know you'll enjoy living in Alberta. The Trent ranch is a great place. As foreman, I can pretty much assure you of a job. We definitely need a good farrier." He grabbed Tom's hand and shook it again.

"Clay! Tom!" Paige ran across the parking lot toward them, waving, her face bright. "Madison's awake! Steve says she'll be all right! Come in! He says we can see her for five minutes!"

"Thank God." Tom turned and started to jog after Paige, who'd turned to run back to the hospital. When he realized Clay wasn't following, he stopped and swung around. "Come on, Clay! The woman you love is awake. Let her see your ugly face!"

"No." He rubbed the back of his aching neck. "I have things to do. I'll see you next month for the mill opening. Keep me posted on Madison's progress, will you?"

An hour later he was in the Piper Cub, rising high over Chemsly. On impulse he circled back and around the old estate. Looking down at the newly repaired barn, he felt an irrational urge to land the plane and head out to the place, to settle himself on an upturned bucket in one of the now vacant stalls with his guitar, and play a sad song with only Patience for company.

****

Madison shifted carefully against the pile of pillows on her mother's couch and flinched. Three weeks since the accident, and she still wasn't back to work. Another two weeks, Dr. McLean declared, and she'd be fine. Still, inactivity wore on her.

She resented the fact that her mother wasn't able to work either. Molly had bills to pay, bills she refused to accept help with. Three weeks of unsalaried leave wasn't helping the situation.

What she couldn't understand was Molly's cheerfulness in spite of everything. Her mother didn't appear to have a worry in the world, financial or otherwise, but when Madison questioned her she got nowhere. Molly would simply smile one of her gentle, enigmatic smiles and tell her she'd understand soon.

"What are you up to, Mom?" she asked as Molly placed a breakfast tray in front of her. "I know that 'cat that swallowed the canary' look. You always had it just before you sprang a surprise birthday party on me...or a special Christmas gift."

"Really? What a clever girl you are. Now eat your eggs." Molly gave her hand a little pat, favored her with one of her most radiant smiles, and left the bedroom.

****

Madison sat in the lawn chair on her mother's front porch, Ceilidh by her side, and took a deep breath of the clean spring afternoon air. The mill, closed for a refit, no longer belched smoke and fumes, while government and military crews were back in the bush cleaning up those polluted ponds. Her entire agenda had been completed. Physically she felt much better; emotionally she should have been on a high. But she wasn't. Not by a long shot.

Although she fought to deny it, she knew the reason. A reason named Clayton Archer. Her mother had told her he came back after her accident, that he stayed in Chemsly until he knew she was out of danger but then left as quickly as he'd come. He hadn't waited around to speak with her.

She couldn't blame him. She'd been less than candid with him about some major events in her past. The admission didn't help.

Her thoughts were interrupted as a familiar black BMW pulled up at the curb. Rick Reid climbed out and came toward her, affable grin in place, a cardboard tray with two coffees in his hand.

"Afternoon, Madison." He came up the steps as Ceilidh barked a greeting. "Hi, Ceilidh girl. Glad someone's happy to see me." Madison let the frown that had furrowed her forehead at recognizing him stay in place.

"What do you want, Rick?"

"A chance to talk, to straighten things out." He

handed her a cup. "I met Molly at the supermarket, and she said you were out here alone. I thought I'd take the opportunity to try to clear the air between us. We've gotta live in the same town, Maddy. Keepin' an old feud goin' now that the reason's gone doesn't make sense. I'd like us to be friends again. Clay's sure as hell buried the hatchet. He reinstated me as manager of the mill last time he was here." He perched on the porch railing and snapped open the tab on his cup.

"He did?" She choked on her first sip of coffee.

"Sure a' shootin'. Seems someone convinced him of my messy but well-intentioned struggle to keep the mill goin'. That wouldn't have been you, now would it, Miss Madison?" He quirked her a crooked grin.

"God, no."

"Ah, well, then maybe he stumbled on those facts all on his lonesome." He ran his hand over a supporting pillar and looked up into the verandah's roof. "You were lucky, bein' brought up in this house with parents like Molly and Dan."

"Don't start down memory lane, Rick." Her tone was hard and brittle. "I know you had a rough time growing up, but that doesn't excuse the nasty innuendo you led Clay Archer to believe about us."

"Movin' on, Madison." He returned his attention to her, becoming deadly serious. "Clay loves you, for God's sake. Nothin' I could ever say or do will change the fact. Call him, make up with him."

"He was the one hurling accusations, not giving me a chance to repudiate them. He's the one who left in a major snit."

"And he's the one who's comin' back to start the wheels rollin' for the rehab site." Rick squinted up into the sun as a Piper Cub crossed the clear blue sky above the house. "Come on, Maddy." He stood and held out a hand. "I'll drive you to the airport."

Ceilidh, catching his enthusiasm, leapt to her feet and barked.

"Now there's a smart gal." He laughed. "Sure, you can come, too. Reckon you're anxious to see Chance again. Come on, Maddy. Time's a wastin', woman."

"No!" She ignored his offer. "He accused me of sleeping with you to get what I wanted. You must have told him one great story, Mr. Reid."

She was all-out furious, ready to breathe fire.

"I never told him any such thing." He stared down at her, his face coldly serious. "I said you filched my keys and searched my office. Anything beyond that was supposition on his part…jealous supposition."

"It doesn't really matter." She settled back in her chair with a weary sigh. "He believed it…thought me capable of it."

"The man is crazy jealous, girl! Hell, I'd react the same way if someone suggested Chrissy was usin' sex to get what she wanted from another man."

"You're that serious about her?" Madison glanced up at him. "I've heard rumors, but…"

"Hell, yes. But don't go changin' the subject, missy. Come on, now. Let's go meet the man. Ceilidh's willin', and she's one clever pooch."

He grinned down at the little dog, and she barked again.

"No. He thought the worst of me. He left. The ball's in his court."

The plane dropped lower in the sky as it headed into the airport.

Rick shrugged and moved away from the railing. "Okay, fine. Make the biggest mistake of your life. You can't say I didn't try to prevent it."

****

The first person Clay saw when he and Chance entered the Chemsly airport was Rick Reid. He sucked in a deep breath and reminded himself that Rick had been forced to do his stepfather's bidding in his efforts to keep the mill open, that the man was now his top executive at the facility. What stuck in his gut was the image of the handsome, rangy man and Madison being intimate.

Forcing those thoughts aside as best he could, he walked toward his affable-looking mill manager. He couldn't hate the man because he'd been attracted to Madison. Any man with a drop of testosterone would be. No, there was only one villain in the scenario and, much as he hated to admit it, her name was Dr. Madison Todd.

"Clay, good to see you, boy." Rick met him halfway across the terminal, hand extended in greeting. "Everything's goin' great at the mill and cleanup site."

"Good, good. Now it's on to the rehab business." When he'd had that coffee shop meeting with Rick and reinstated him as mill manager, he'd been able to deal with the gaunt, stubble-faced man. But now the man was back to his former attractive, good-natured, handsome self. Wearing casual grey pants and a green silk shirt and looking as freshly groomed as if he'd just had a shave, shower, and haircut, Rick Reid could catch any woman's eye.

"You're still thinkin' you'd like to punch my lights out?" Rick's astute reading of his mind caught him unawares.

"Yeah. Do you blame me?" There was no answer but the honest one.

"No." Rick shook his head slowly and looked down at his shining black shoes. "Not when you insist on believin' what you do about me and Maddy. But, damn it, Clay"—he looked at him, eyes bright with sincerity—"it's not true. We dated a few times. I drank a bit too much one night, fell asleep, and she took the opportunity to steal my keys and go through my wallet. When I realized what she'd done, I got mad as hell and swore I'd get back at her for it. But that was it. No sleepin' together, not even a half-decent kiss. Give me a Bible. I'll swear on it."

"Yeah?"

"Yeah, God's truth. Maddy Todd is a lady, just like her mom. She takes that kind of thing real serious. She had one guy in all her years in Chemsly, and that was Tom Mills. That's not the MO of a woman who sleeps around…for any reason."

"Good to know." Clay hefted the duffel bag he'd let slip to the floor while they'd talked. "But she still used me."

"Yeah, well, maybe in the beginnin'…before she got to know you." Rick fell into step with him as he headed toward the terminal door. "But later…"

"Later, after she'd got what she wanted, she was ready to move on. I'll bet that doctor she had a thing for in Africa got the same deal, not the other way around like she told it."

"Hey!" Rick stopped and grabbed Clay's arm to pull him to an abrupt halt. "Maddy's no liar. Stubborn, determined, irritatin' as hell when she thinks it's in a good cause, but no liar. I've known her all of my life, cowboy, and a whole lot better than you."

"You gonna deck me?" Clay faced him, a slow grin spreading across his face.

"Naw." Rick hesitated, then released him and grinned back. "My work here is done. That look you've got plastered across your face tells me that, if nothin' else, I've started you thinkin' again. Now let's go. There's a bar in the mall that serves great T-bones, and a couple of 'em have our names on them."

"Sounds good." They started off together.

"Maybe later we can swing by Molly's house and see if Maddy is still sittin' on the verandah."

"Take it easy, man. I'm not ready for that...yet. I have to think."

As they headed out into the parking lot in a sudden spring shower, Clay knew that although he believed Rick about the extent of his relationship with Madison, a little four-letter word would continue to haunt him. "Used" didn't easily erase itself from a man's mind.

****

"Morning, Paige." Clay doffed his Stetson as Madison's sister opened the kitchen door of her home.

"Clay, hello. What a nice surprise. Come in." She stepped back to allow him in. "The place is a mess. I just took the twins to school and haven't had time to tidy up." She gestured to the breakfast remains scattered over the table.

"Looks like a home ought to look." He grinned, fingering his hat.

"Please. Take a seat. Coffee?" She indicated the percolator.

"Sounds good, but only if you'll agree to have one

with me. Paige, I've come with a proposition."

He sat down at the table as she shoved aside a half-empty cereal bowl to make room for his cup.

"I can't imagine what that could be." She took a chair opposite him. "But you've got me interested."

"I want you to be the CFO for Glendon Forest Products."

"What?" She blinked wide blue eyes, and Clay thought how pretty all the Todd women were.

"I want you to manage the financial aspects of my company." He drew a deep breath and continued. "Previously, my stepfather did most of that work. From the time of his illness until now, Rick and Chrissy have been doing a slap-up job of it. Now I want it done properly, by a professional. I'm willing to pay the going rate for such services, even more."

"I don't know what to say." Paige looked down into her cup, and he saw confusion registered in her expression. "I didn't take the job I was interviewed for the day we got Madison out of jail. They offered it to me, but I still wasn't sure…"

"Jordan wouldn't have to take all that overtime, with you helping out financially." He pressed his case. "And I can take the kids out to the estate if you get stuck for day care from time to time."

"You're offering to babysit?"

"Sure, why not? It would be fun to have them around. I could buy them ponies…"

"And spoil them terribly." She was smiling as she looked up at him. "All right. I'll have to discuss it with Jordan first, of course, but from my perspective I'm willing to give it a try."

****

"Come on, you two. I have to turn you over to your mother or she won't let me babysit for you again." Clay led the pair, one at each hand, into the mill office area.

Paige looked up from her desk, a wide smile lighting up her face. "Hey, guys, what have you and Uncle Clay been up to?"

"We went riding," Daniel blurted out as Katie ran to hug her mom. "My pony's name is Doodle and Katie's is Bug."

"Clay, you didn't." Paige stood and gave him an admonishing look.

"They needed a home…found them at the SPCA." He tried to contain the grin the children's pleasure was forcing across his face.

"Oh, so it was just a good deed…nothing to do with having two little pressure cookers wanting them?"

"Well, they do have birthdays coming up…"

"Mom, Mom, you've got to come out to Uncle Clay's and see them!" Daniel was pulling on her hand.

"I suppose I will." She took her suit jacket from the back of the chair and picked up her purse. "Now, how about you two running into the lunchroom next door and getting cookies and milk from Anna? She's expecting you. I want to talk to Uncle Clay for a few minutes."

"Sure." The pair darted off as Paige shrugged into her jacket.

"Well?" Clay looked at her. "How goes it?"

"Very well. Clay, I've discovered a number of hidden accounts where your stepfather squirreled away large sums of money. If you were concerned about having enough to build the rehab center after the mill refit, worry no more. By my reckoning, there's enough

233

to build a state-of-the-art facility, and lots left over."

He stared at her for a moment, then let out a cowboy whoop and caught her up in his arms.

"Paige Anderson, you're a miracle worker!"

"Uncle Clay, Mom, are you okay?" Daniel appeared in the doorway, a glass of milk in one hand, a large chocolate chip cookie in the other.

"We're fine, Daniel." Paige smiled and adjusted her jacket as Clay released her. "Your uncle has just received some very good news."

Chapter Eighteen

In a big vacant field a mile from the center of Chemsly, on a sunny, warm May afternoon, a crowd gathered in a circle around the mayor and town representatives. Several reporters and a TV crew stood ready to capture the event about to unfold.

"Ladies and gentlemen," Mayor Sam Elliot said into a microphone. "Before we get to the actual ground-breaking ceremony that will mark the commencement of the Abby Archer-Gregory Rehab Centre, I'd like to take this opportunity to express our thanks on behalf of all the citizens of Chemsly to the man who made this day possible. Without the power of his vision and his generous financial support, this wonderful facility would never have come to our community. Now, please, put your hands together for our benefactor, Clayton Archer."

There was a spontaneous burst of applause as Clay stepped up to the microphone to shake Sam Elliot's hand. When the mayor stepped aside, Clay raised his hand, and quiet returned as cameras snapped and TV crews swung into action.

"Thanks for coming out today to mark this occasion." He looked out over the crowd, hoping his appreciation of their attendance was reflected in his expression. "My mother would have been really glad to meet you. Although during the years she spent in this community she was seldom an active member of it, I know that, given the opportunity, she would have enjoyed getting to know each and every one of you."

There was a respectful sprinkling of applause. Clay knew he didn't have to elaborate further. Most people in the crowd understood the circumstances that had prevented her from participating in town activities and friendships.

"Now, before we continue with the ceremony, I'd like to make an announcement and introduce you to my new CFO—chief financial officer, that is—Paige Anderson." He turned and extended a hand to draw Paige into place beside him. Enthusiastic applause broke out. Tom stuck his fingers between his lips and whistled. Standing beside the farrier, Jordan hoisted Katie up to better see her mother, while Tom provided the same service for Daniel.

"Thank you." Paige smiled at the gathering. "Although I never dreamed I'd be in this position, I'm delighted."

She stepped back amid more applause as Daniel yelled, "Go, Mom!"

"Now to other business." Clay spoke again. "The ground-breaking. For this job, I've asked a lady you all know and respect, the lady who has graciously consented to be the administrative director of this new facility, Mrs. Molly Todd. Rick, will you hand Mrs. Todd the shovel?"

A wild outburst of clapping accompanied Molly's move forward. She looked fresh as a summer's day in a pale beige pantsuit, a pink scarf at her throat, as she accepted the beribboned spade from a pleased-as-punch-looking Rick Reid.

"Make the dirt fly, Miss Molly." A ripple of laughter ran through the crowd at the mill manager's remark.

Rick was still a favorite among the residents, since Clay had been careful not to reveal the depths of his mill manager's cover-up in the pollution problem. Now that a remedy was nearing completion, he saw no reason to crucify the man. Overall, Rick had been an excellent mill manager, and Clay knew he would need the man's skill of knowing the business from the bottom up to keep the plant operational on a profit level that would support the rehab center.

As he watched Molly sink the shovel into the earth at the previously prepared spot, he caught himself thinking how lovely she was and that Madison when she reached her mother's age would look much the same. Once upon a time he'd thought he'd like to be the guy who reached sixty or seventy or ninety by her side. He'd thought he could never get enough of Dr. Madison Todd. But that wasn't going to happen. Proof was in the fact that she'd apparently chosen not to attend the ceremony that day.

He snapped back to the moment as Molly laid aside a shovelful of dirt and the crowd burst into loud appreciation.

****

"Clay, will you walk with me…down to that lovely brook at the back of this beautiful property?"

Molly touched Clay's arm as he finished a conversation with one of the town's council members. He was standing beside the refreshment table that had been set up to mark the conclusion of the ground-breaking ceremony, a coffee in his hand.

"Sure." He put it down and glanced at her pastel pumps. "But in those shoes? Could be the ground's still pretty soft down there at this time of year."

"Don't worry about the shoes. This is important."

"Okay." He'd learned better than to argue with any Todd woman when she got that determined look on her face. He took her arm, and they strolled away from the crowd.

When they reached the point where the brook gushed across a corner of the property, Molly stopped him.

"This is lovely, Clay." She gazed at the stream frolicking through a small grove of white birch. "We'll be able to bring patients out here on fine days to enjoy nature. I've always had a theory that the beauty of the outdoors has a powerful restorative ability."

"I'm glad you suggested this property. My mother would have liked it here. I wouldn't have found it without your help. It wasn't listed with any of the realtors I consulted. With your permission, I'd like to call this area the Daniel Todd Memorial Park."

"Oh, Clay!" Molly's blue eyes filled with tears. "How perfectly lovely! And so thoughtful. Dan would feel very honored…as do I."

"Well…" He glanced away, embarrassed by her heartfelt reaction. "It wouldn't have happened if you hadn't found it for me."

"Helps to be acquainted with most of the local people. Incidentally, Steven has found a replacement for me. I'll be able to take up my position with your company by the end of the month."

"Great. I'll need your expertise in purchasing equipment, hiring staff, even in assisting with design features. Do you mind?"

"Mind! It will be a dream come true to be able to bring to life some of the ideas I've had over my years in nursing."

"Good, I'm glad. Now, we should be getting back. Your shoes look damp. I don't want my administrator catching cold." He started to turn her back toward the gathering near the road, but she stopped him.

"Clay, I didn't invite you down here to discuss the center." She looked up at him. He saw the same steely determination in her eyes he'd so often seen in Madison's—and heaved a sigh.

"Okay, Molly, let's have it."

"It's about Madison…"

"What? What is it? I thought she'd recovered. Molly…" His impassioned response was reflexive.

"Calm down, dear. She has recovered…physically. Mentally and emotionally, well, that's another matter."

"Yeah, well, she put herself under quite a strain these past few months, what with her mill campaign and her practice, and now she's recovering from a serious accident."

"Yes, but that's not what I want to talk about. I want to talk about you and her and the huge mistake you're both making by remaining apart now that the barrier between you is gone."

"You mean the mill. Ah, Molly, it's not the mill. It's…"

"The men in her past? Tom Mills and Dr. Jason Kenny?" She continued to look up at him, eyes soft but intent. "Maybe even Rick Reid?"

"Yeah, well, Tom Mills I understand. He's a good guy. Dr. Kenny—I just know he hurt her to the bone, and I'd like a chance for a real good swing at him. It's Rick I can't get over. She used him to get what she needed…like she used me."

"No, no, no!" Molly caught him by the arm and peered urgently up into his face. "Oh, I won't deny she had other plans for you. But not for long. I recognized the signs long before she did. That's one of the reasons I invited you to Thanksgiving dinner. I wanted the pair of you to meet in a congenial setting. I saw then it wouldn't work until the problem at the mill was solved, so I let it go…for a while. Now that obstacle's gone. It's time you both did the sensible thing and admitted you're in love."

"She's not interested, Molly."

"Have you tried…since the mill problem has been resolved?"

"Yeah, well, sort of…at Christmas. But she ran away so fast she left one shoe behind."

"Now look here, my boy." Molly seized him by the arm, blue eyes blazing. "I was married to a wonderful man for nearly forty years. We were in love and lovers every single one of them. It's always been my fondest wish that my daughters would have a similar experience. One already has. Now I plan to see that the other is similarly blessed. Do you hear me, Clayton Archer?"

"Yes, ma'am."

"Then get to it, my boy. This cupid is getting cold, wet feet."

"Yes, ma'am." A grin had broken out over his face as she lectured him, and he couldn't resist teasing her just a little.

Her words were making him more hopeful and

happier than he'd expected to be, even on this special day. It appeared his two fondest dreams were about to come true…if he could just convince Dr. Madison Todd to go along with one of them.

Clay bent and gave Molly a kiss on the cheek.

"Never mind all that." She brushed him aside in pretended annoyance. "You can thank me properly after you've convinced my daughter to marry you. It will take a bit of underhandedness. You'll have to do exactly as I say."

"Okay. Set up your plan, and I'll follow along."

****

"Rick, can I see you for a minute…alone?"

Rick Reid turned from where he'd been helping Chrissy gather up paper cups and plates.

"Sure, Boss." He paused to give Chrissy a quick kiss on the cheek. "Be right back, baby."

She flashed him a glowing smile.

Something definitely going on there. The thought hit Clay as Rick joined him to stroll across the deserted field.

"Nothing wrong at the mill, is there?"

"No, no, everything is fine. And you're going to keep it that way. This is personal. I want to congratulate you. I hope you and Chrissy will be very happy."

"Shows, does it?"

"Pretty hard to miss."

"Yeah, well, I figure it's got to be serious. I've been lookin' at houses and picturin' her in a white dress. Corny, right? Maybe even crazy, considerin' the mess my folks made of their marriage."

"My mother didn't have a terrific marriage, the second time around. But that's not going to stop me.

I've been seeing another lady in one of those get-ups almost since the first day I met her. I was even visualizing her helping me fix up that monstrosity of a house I own."

"Maybe we'd both better get started workin' on those projects, just in case we get lucky and they want to be June brides. Actually"—Rick dug in his pocket and pulled out a small box—"I think I may just have a head start on you, Boss." He snapped it open to display a ring bearing an emerald surrounded by diamonds. "Her birthstone is an emerald. What do you think?"

"Nice, very nice. Good luck, Rick. When are you planning to make the big move?"

"Tonight. I've booked a table at a restaurant with a view of the river. I'll keep you posted."

Whistling, Rick stuffed the box into his pocket and started back toward where the caterers were folding up tables and Chrissy was waiting beside Molly.

Okay, now I'd better find out exactly what my future mother-in-law has up her sleeve.

****

"Mom, what are you doing here? And who is that?" Astonished, Molly stared as her mother stepped out onto the cabin's verandah, a small sand-colored puppy in her arms. Molly Todd's smile was so bright it challenged the beauty of the spring morning. Madison had known something unusual was in the air when her mother had insisted on meeting her up at the cabin.

"I'm the lady of this house…again," she said. "This is Sandy, my new friend. He's going to live with me."

"Lady of the house…?" Madison stood beside her Jeep and could only stare as Ceilidh bounded out the vehicle door she'd left hanging open and raced up the cabin's steps. The little dog paused for a moment and stood on her hind legs to sniff the newcomer in Molly's arms before she rushed to the screen door and barked. An answering yelp startled Madison. She recognized it.

The door swung open to let an exuberant Chance greet Ceilidh with licks and leaps. Behind the gleeful pair, Clay Archer emerged, wearing his Stetson and cowboy boots and dangling in his hand a black strappy sandal she recognized. He paused.

"I'll leave you two to talk." Molly glanced from one to the other. She put the puppy down, clicked a lead on his collar, and headed down the steps. "Sandy needs a little exercise, and it will give him a chance to get to know Chance and Ceilidh."

With a smug, self-satisfied smile, she turned and headed toward the lake, the three dogs dancing around her.

Madison came out of her trance and slammed the door of her vehicle shut. "Why is Mom here? More to the point, why are you here?"

He swung the shoe by a strap and grinned. "Prince Charming seeking Cinderella."

"Really." The word reeked of sarcasm.

"Yeah, really. Also, the mill is ready to re-open next week, and construction will be starting on the Rehab Center. I had to come." Madison tried to ignore how sexy and handsome he looked. And failed.

"And those two facts are connected to my mother, a puppy, and this place, how?"

She was struggling to sound detached, even annoyed, but her heart was pounding like that of a teenager hoping for an invitation to her first prom.

"I was checking up with the director of the rehab center," he replied. "As you probably already know, your mother has agreed to take on the position. This place and Sandy are a signing bonus. My boss at the ranch, Jim Trent, tells me it's a perfectly acceptable hiring practice, necessary if you want to get the best people."

"So you've gotten everything you wanted." She struggled for sarcasm, but her mother's face, bright with happiness for the first time since her father's death, kept appearing in her mind to ruin the attempt.

"So did you…apparently. The mill's been refurbished with state-of-the-art pollution control devices, and that toxic pond has been safely drained." He drew a deep breath.

"Great place, this," he continued, looking around. "I expect you'll want to spend a lot of time up here…maybe with that doctor friend from Africa, when he resurfaces."

"It's Jason Kenny, and he definitely won't be resurfacing. Ceilidh!" she called. "We have to be leaving."

"Wait." He came down the steps and walked across the yard to confront her.

"What?" She paused, her hand on the Jeep's door handle, and was appalled to discover her heart rate upping with every long-legged stride he took toward her. She'd thought he couldn't be as handsome and sexy as she remembered. But he was, even more so.

"I wish you hadn't." He stopped two feet in front of her and looked down at her, blue eyes intense and unflinching.

"Hadn't what?" She frowned, confused.

"Damn it, Madison, I wish you hadn't used me."

"Oh, Clay, I may have at first, but not later...not later." She looked up at him, eyes wide with regret.

"Yeah, well, that's a little hard to believe, given..." He stopped and stared up into the budding branches above her head.

"Given what? Rick Reid's description of my romantic past?" Anger mixed with sexual tension raged through every inch of her body. "I admit I used him to gain access to the mill's files, and that I tried to use you in the beginning. I also admit Tommy and I went steady in high school and that he tried to start up again when I moved back here. But I'll also tell you it was over for me. You can believe it or not!"

"Because of that doctor in Africa, right?"

"No, because I realized I'd never be able to accept him as anyone more than a friend." Her tone softened, emotions draining her fervor, making her suddenly weak.

"What about...?"

"Dr. Jason Kenny?" She looked up at him, and suddenly her eyes were swimming with tears. "If you must know, *he* used *me*. I was only a distraction until he could return to Canada and hook up with another woman he could exploit...to advance his career. Satisfied?"

She swung away from him and again tried to open the Jeep's door, but his hand shot out to keep it shut.

"You can't deny Prince Charming a chance to at least give this thing a try." He dangled the sandal in front of her, irresistible grin in place. "Come on." He led her to the cabin steps. "Sit...please."

"Okay, okay. I can see you're determined to play

out this ridiculous farce." She could barely muster a semblance of annoyance, her heart was beating so hard.

Damn it, he's the cowboy version of Prince Charming, and the man is taking my breath away.

He removed her running shoe and sock, then paused to run his hand gently over her bare instep.

Oh, my God!

"Just get on with it." She was caving…fast.

"Ah, ha!" He slid the shoe into place. "A perfect fit." He looked up at her with those killer blue eyes and she lost it…completely.

"Oh, Clay."

How much was a woman supposed to take and remain cold and unaffected?

She jumped up, lopsided in one high-heeled sandal and one sneaker, into his arms.

"I've missed you, Dr. Todd," he breathed against her hair. "Man, I've missed you."

"And I've missed you."

"I wanted to come back, I wanted…"

"Why didn't you?"

"After what I said last fall?" He drew her out from him and looked down at her. "I couldn't risk it until the mill had been renovated."

"And you could give my mother a puppy and a job, and this place? Seems like overkill, cowboy."

"Dr. Todd, I love you. Nothing is too much to win you over. And, by the way, Don Quixote has always been one of my favorite fictional characters."

"Paige gave you her 'tilting at windmills' speech, didn't she?"

She looked up at him, teasingly indignant.

"As a matter of fact, yes, she did. But what would

the world be if it weren't for dragon and windmill slayers? One pretty dull place, I'm thinking."

He leaned forward to kiss her on the tip of her nose.

"What about Alberta? When will you be heading back there?"

"In a week or two, to finish off some work, gather up my stuff, and arrange to ship my horse to Chemsly. It'll be a whole lot easier for me to bring Apache here than to move you and Candy and Scout and Ceilidh and Patience and her family out west. And I want to be near your family for Christmas…and all such future events. That means a lot to me. That is, if you're going to give me a reason to hang around, maybe volunteer to help me fix up my monstrosity of a house, and…"

"I'll give you a reason." Her voice became soft and sensuous. "Oh my, yes, I'll give you a reason, cowboy."

He pulled off his Stetson and lowered his head to kiss her. It was some time before she allowed him to surface.

"Come back to Alberta with me while I finish up out there." He held her out to look down at her. "I'd like you to meet a man who's been like a father to me. His name is Jim Trent."

"Lacey's father?"

"Yeah, Lacey's father."

"Won't he be annoyed that you're leaving? How will he replace you?"

"Oh, I think he'll find a good replacement in Tom Mills. And it's high time Miss Lacey started taking over the financial end of things. They'll make a great pair of ranchers."

"But aren't you afraid you might find Chemsly dull

after running a cattle ranch?"

"Dull? With you around, Doctor? Hardly. What about you? I won't be a cowboy anymore...Paige did warn me about your fantasies. I'll simply be overseeing the mill and the rehab center, and working at the estate. Oh, and I wear reading glasses. Think you can handle that mundane kind of guy?"

"I can handle anything, cowboy or CEO. Just give me a chance to show you. But in case you feel in need of one more project, there's this horrendous puppy mill about forty miles south of town that absolutely has to be shut down."

He hesitated, remembering the day of the fire, when he'd climbed into that rattletrap of an airplane to do what he felt was right, and remembered she hadn't tried to stop him. He drew a deep breath.

"Yeah, sure, of course. We'll get right on it."

"And maybe once in a while you can dress up in jeans and boots and a Stetson." She slanted him a sly look. "A girl likes to live out her fantasies from time to time."

"Will do. And no more hair straightening. A man likes to have his, too."

As he drew her back into his arms he had a sudden vision of whirling wooden blades and giant, fire-breathing lizards, and he knew his life with Dr. Madison Todd would never be dull. He also knew he was about to become part of her family, the kind of family he'd longed for all of his life.

A word about the author...

Award-winning author of thirty-four published books, Gail is a graduate of Queen's University and lives in New Brunswick, Canada, with her husband and with Fancy, her Little River Duck Dog.

Visit her at:

macgail@nbnet.nb.ca